SUNCHASER'S QUEST

Read all the Unicorns of Balinor books:

Unicorns of Balinor

Sunchaser's Quest

Mary Stanton

AN
APPLE
PAPERBACK

SCHOLASTIC INC.
New York Toronto London Auckland Sydney
Mexico City New Delhi Hong Kong

For John Robert,
from his loving Mary.

Cover illustration by D. Craig

ISBN 0-439-06281-0

12 11 10 9 8 7 6 5 4 3 2 1   9/9 0 1 2 3 4/0

Printed in the U.S.A.   40
First Scholastic printing, May 1999

1

It was a beautiful day in the Celestial Valley. The sun was at its height over the deep green meadows. A soft breeze rustled the leaves of the sapphire willow trees lining the banks of the Imperial River. The unicorns of the Celestial Valley herd grazed peacefully in the sunshine, each unicorn a flare of brilliant color corresponding to a color of the rainbow. A beautiful violet unicorn with a silver mane and tail gazed down upon the herd from the Eastern Ridge. This was Atalanta, the Dreamspeaker, mate to Numinor, the Golden One, and counselor to the herd. Her deep violet eyes were troubled. Sorrow had come to the Celestial Valley. The herd's ancient enemies were stirring. The threat of war loomed.

Atalanta sighed deeply. In normal times, today would be the first day of training the Dreamspeaker's Disciple. She had already selected a candidate, Devi, a weanling unicorn who already showed the spirit of adventure necessary for the hard life of Dreamspeakers. But she had spoken to Nana, the Herd Caretaker, and told her to cancel Devi's first lesson. These were hard times, and she had to consult with Numinor about what lay ahead.

Atalanta turned and went up the Eastern Ridge to the Cave of Numinor. Below her, the unicorns grazed under the sun. The adults formed a protective circle around the nursery. The babies were a spot of silver-gray right in the middle of the herd. Devi the weanling unicorn looked up and watched as Atalanta disappeared around a curve of the Eastern Ridge. Nana, the Caretaker, had just told him he couldn't meet with the Dreamspeaker for his first lesson, and he was trying to hide his disappointment. "But *why* can't I study with the Dreamspeaker?" he asked in his high, sweet voice. He was careful not to whine. "I've been good."

"You know that the Dreamspeaker has very important matters to attend to," Nana said. Nana was a pleasant, rosy sort of pink. Her horn was a creamy ivory, as were her mane and tail. She was round and soft to nestle up to. "And you know that she always keeps her word. She'll get to your lessons soon, Devi. Just not today."

"Then can I go play?"

Nana sighed. Like all baby unicorns, Devi was a pearly gray color, which would deepen to a rainbow color as the unicorn grew into adulthood. Nana was sure what color Devi would be as a yearling: chocolate-brown with an obsidian horn. Chocolate-brown was the stubbornest color Nana could think of, and obsidian was the hardest jewel. Devi was the stubbornest foal she'd handled in a long, long time. When Devi began his apprenticeship to Atalanta this kind of determination would be good. But for now, it made things difficult. "I don't think you should play today. Why don't you take a nice nap with the others?"

Devi pouted. "I'm not sleepy!"

"You *should* be wantin' a nice rest. If you run around too much, you'll get hot. And if you get hot, you could get sunstroke. And if you get sunstroke, I'll have a conniption. You wouldn't want that."

Since Devi didn't know what a conniption was, he didn't care. Devi didn't think his chances of tiptoeing away for a little adventure without permission were too good, either. Someone would spot him right away.

"If I can't play, can I just walk down to the river?"

Nana pushed out her lower lip. She hated to say no. And she hated to think that it wouldn't be safe. The Celestial Valley had been a haven for her and her kind forever. Until now. For the past three days, the herd had been alive with the terrible news: Entia was on the prowl! Entia, the Shifter, was the enemy of all those in the Celestial Valley and the lands of humans beneath it. He had kidnapped the King and Queen of Balinor, and threatened the life of the

Princess Arianna and the Sunchaser, her Bonded unicorn. Atalanta and Numinor had sent Arianna and the Sunchaser through the Gap to safety at Glacier River Farm, with the help of the loyal villagers of Balinor.

But the haven of the farm had proved to be a trap. Arianna's memory was gone, obliterated by the Shifter's tricks. Ari no longer knew that she was the Princess of Balinor. And worse yet was the condition of the Sunchaser himself. With his horn hacked off in the heat of the battle at the Shifter's Palace, he, too, had lost his memory: He no longer knew he was the Sunchaser, Lord of the Animals in Balinor, and Bonded to the Princess Arianna.

And now the Shifter stalked Balinor — and perhaps the Celestial Valley itself! No, it wasn't safe for little Devi to travel to the river. She shook her head. "I don't think a walk would be a good idea, either."

Devi rubbed his little horn against Nana's foreleg, then nibbled her pink whiskers. "Please?" he said. "I'll be very, very careful."

Nana's lower lip still stuck out. Devi blew softly against her cheek. "I won't go in the water," he promised. "And I'll be very, very, VERY careful."

Nana looked at the meadows filled with unicorns, all within shouting distance if trouble came. She looked at the sky, a clear, deep violet-blue that rivaled the color of the Dreamspeaker's eyes. And Devi was such a rowdy little foal! If he took a walk —

just a short one! — it might tire him out enough so that she could nap a little herself this afternoon. "All right," Nana said. She blew back at him, a soft tickle of breath that made him sneeze. "But you come right back here."

"Hoo-ray!" Devi jumped into the air. Nana chuckled as she watched him trot off. Young unicorns' knees were so knobby when they were small! And their little tails and manes were nothing more than soft fuzz. She bent her head to graze, looking up occasionally to see Devi skipping down to the Imperial River. Then young Lydiana got into a shoving match with Viola-Rose, who'd just barely been weaned, and Nana forgot all about Devi as she settled the squabble.

Devi slowed from a skip to a walk as he approached the banks of the Imperial River. He looked back. Nana was paying more attention to the spat between Lydiana and Viola-Rose than she was to him.

Good. He was safe to explore. He danced a little in the short sweet grass. The trees dropped flowers on the rippling water. Sunlight sparkled off the wavelets. Everything was peaceful.

Peaceful enough for *adventure*.

Devi was upset about the lost Princess. And even more upset about the terrible accident to the great bronze unicorn Sunchaser. A unicorn without his horn! And one who didn't know who he was!

Devi thought, Why not just *tell* them?

Tell the Princess that she's the Princess. Tell Chase that he's the Sunchaser, the mightiest of the Royal unicorns in Balinor and the Lord of the Animals there. And once they were told? Well! The animals in Balinor wouldn't lose their ability to talk and everything would be all right!

Devi stood in the sunshine and formed a plan. He'd been to the Watching Pool, the magical spot that allowed the Dreamspeaker to see events in lands below the Celestial Valley.

He didn't need lessons to be a Dreamspeaker! He could go to the pool, call up the Princess and the Sunchaser, and tell them who they really were! Then they would fight the evil Shifter and everything would be back to normal.

Devi followed the course of the river up the hill, stopping to nibble at a bit of grass, then to nose a pebble along the well-marked path, just in case Nana was looking to see what he was doing. His alert ears caught the sound of falling water, and he trotted a little faster to reach the source. He rounded a large amethyst boulder and heaved a sigh of relief. The Watching Pool!

He stood before the wide pool of clear water surrounded by amethyst rock. Water rushed over the lip of the pool and into the Imperial River. This was the Watching Pool. Devi knew all about it. Every unicorn did. The Watching Pool was where the Celestial herd watched events in the world of humans. But Devi had never been there alone before.

The wind stirred the brush at the side of the pool. The air felt hot. Suddenly, his plan to call Princess Arianna and the Sunchaser through the Watching Pool seemed — dangerous.

He crept nearer.

No one yelled, "Halt!" or "Stop!" or worse yet — "Back to the nursery, little one!" He stuck out his chest and pranced a bit to give himself courage. He was not a little one. He was Devi the Great!

The water fell with the sound of silver bells.

He took one hesitant step, then another, until he reached the broad shelf of amethyst where Atalanta the Dreamspeaker stood each morning to gaze at events in the world of humans. The rock was worn smooth from the hooves of Dreamspeakers standing watch throughout time.

"Ho," Devi said as he bent over his reflection in the water. And, "Ho" again as he saw his own face — tiny horn, wide green eyes, and frizzy forelock.

He could do it! He could call Princess Arianna and the Sunchaser! "I am Devi! The Great!" he piped in his high, sweet voice. He bent his head. Just as he'd seen the Dreamspeaker do, he touched his horn to the water, once, twice, three times. "I call Arianna, Princess of Balinor!"

He stepped back. The water began to spin and darken. With a sudden shudder, the waters convulsed and went black. A sickly yellow-green light glowed eerily in its depths. A terrible odor of decay drifted from the surface. Devi swallowed hard.

"Devi!" came a cross, gruff voice. "Get out o' there, bud!"

Devi jumped into the air. A stout black-and-white unicorn regarded him balefully from the upper slope of the hill. Tobiano, the rudest unicorn in the herd. He didn't like foals at all. Devi tripped and scrambled helplessly against the smooth rock and fell into the pool with a splash.

Devi had never felt fear in his entire short life. But he felt it now. The waters closed over his head. And they were hot — burning hot! He struggled to breathe and gasped, choking on the taste of ash. The evil yellow-green light surrounded him, blinding him.

And then . . . *skeletal hands on his pasterns, pulling him down!*

He screamed, inhaled more fiery water, and, too scared to think, fell into blackness.

He woke to a cool violet light and the scent of roses. He lay still for a moment, blinking, glorying in the sunshine that warmed his withers, in the feel of the soft breeze against his flanks. He was safe on the banks of the Watching Pool. And he'd have to be thankful to the bossiest unicorn in the herd for pulling him out. Well, he didn't care. He was just glad to be alive.

"Well, then, little Devi." Atalanta's voice was gentle, with a crystal chime. Atalanta, the Dreamspeaker! She had saved him! And that cranky Toby was just behind her! Devi gasped, then stumbled upright as fast as he could. "Oh, Atalanta!" he said miserably. He hung his head. "I just . . . I just wanted to help."

"Ah." Atalanta pricked her ears forward and gazed at him with her deep violet eyes.

"Interferin' little one," Toby grumbled. "Send him back to his ma, I say."

"He's very brave, to try to warn Arianna," Atalanta said. "But Devi, do you know what almost happened to you?"

He shook his head.

"The Shifter was after you!"

Devi's eyes grew round.

"Were you scared?" she asked gently.

He thought about this. He was brave. Atalanta herself had said so, and what she said was true. He puffed out his chest a little, took a breath, then caught that deep purple gaze. "Yes." He scraped one forefoot along the ground.

Atalanta nodded. "Wise, as well as brave," she said. "Those were the hands of Entia himself, pulling you down."

"The Shifter." Devi shuddered.

"And now you know why we have a rule about the Watching Pool, Devi. I, and I alone may call at the pool. Because you never know who — or what — will answer."

9

"I'm sorry." Devi looked up at her. "But Atalanta. Why don't you just tell the Princess who she is? Why don't you help the Sunchaser get his horn back?"

Atalanta bowed her head. Her silky mane flowed over her face, like a light cloud across the sun. "I am doing what I am allowed to do. There is only so much magic to use, and a very few times that I can use it. I am about to use some now. Perhaps you would care to help?"

Devi nodded vigorously. "Oh, yes!"

"Then stand here, next to me."

Devi pranced forward. Then, suddenly shy as the silvery light around Atalanta enveloped him, he dropped his head and stared at his hooves. The left fore was a little chipped, and he rubbed his nose on it furiously. What if she noticed!

But Atalanta was not looking at Devi's hooves. She nodded at Toby. "Are you ready?"

"Guess so," Toby said gruffly. Devi could hear the excitement in his voice.

"Devi?"

He looked up at the Dreamspeaker.

"I am going to open the water. Toby and I are going to Balinor. I will come back alone, for I will not be allowed to stay too long. But Toby will remain there and report to me. I have made arrangements to . . ." She paused, clearly amused at something. "To hook him up with a friend, so to speak."

"How come *you* have to come back? I mean, aren't you the Dreamspeaker?" Devi asked.

"She holds the Deep Magic," Toby said. "It will leave her if she stays too long below. Now me, I have practically no magic at all." He thought a moment.

"Enough," Atalanta said. "Be silent, both of you." She walked to the edge of the pool and struck the water three times with her horn. The water swirled, and Devi held his breath. A vision appeared in the pool of a bronze-haired girl with eyes the color of the sky, and a great bronze horse. A huge collie walked with them. "The Princess, the Sunchaser, and that dog, Lincoln," Atalanta said. "They have just come through the Gap. They are headed to Balinor itself."

"Who's *that?*" Toby grumbled. "That blond kid. How did she get through the Gap?"

"Her name is Lori Carmichael," the Dreamspeaker said thoughtfully. "How odd." She shook herself briskly. "Well, we shall see." She backed away from the pool and raised her head to the sun. Slowly, she rose on her hindquarters until her forelegs reached into the sky. She took a long breath and sang a single note, low, sweet, and throbbing. The waters in the pool parted slowly, as if giant hands were pushing them aside.

The song gathered in strength until Devi closed his eyes with the power of it. When he opened his eyes again, the Dreamspeaker and Toby were gone. Devi leaned over the pool. In the depths, he saw a tiny silver star speeding toward Balinor, and a black-and-white shadow bouncing beside it.

The Dreamspeaker and Toby were on their way to Balinor.

2

ri, Lori Carmichael, and Chase stopped at
the edge of a small field of short grass dotted with
flowers. Lincoln, the collie, stood at Ari's side.

"This is your fault," Lori said flatly.

Ari looked at Lori in exasperation. The blond
girl was a spoiled brat, no doubt about it. She
thought she was the most important riding student
at Glacier River Farm. And unfortunately she was —
but only because of her father's money.

Lori scowled and stamped her feet. "I said
this is your fault! What are you going to do about it?"

"Just let me think a minute." Ari ran her
hands through her hair. She didn't have any idea
where they were or how they'd gotten here. The last
thing she remembered was a frantic ride on Chase
from Glacier River Farm to the safety of the cave in
the south pasture. But the cave hadn't been safe at
all. Some terrible force had pulled her, her dog, and

her horse through a tunnel to this place. And that force had also caught Lori and pulled her through.

"None of this would have happened if you'd just let Chase alone," Ari said, trying to keep her voice reasonable. "You didn't have any business trying to lease him. He's mine!"

"What good is a horse to you?" Lori asked rudely. "Your legs got so messed up from that accident that you can't ride him as much as he needs to be ridden anyway."

Ari rubbed her right calf. Both legs had been broken, in what her foster parents, Ann and Frank, had told her was a truck accident. Chase himself had also been hurt; he still carried a white scar in the middle of his forehead from the tragedy. But Ari was healing just fine. She just couldn't remember anything before the accident. Nothing about Glacier Farm was familiar — not even her foster parents. Chase, her horse, was her only memory. "You just had to have my horse, didn't you? I shouldn't have to remind you, Lori, that if you hadn't chased after us, you'd be safe at the farm."

"I wouldn't have had to chase after you if you'd kept up your end of the bargain!"

"I didn't make the bargain. My foster father did. Because we needed the money to pay my medical bills!"

"Oh, shut up," Lori said. "Just shut up! And get us of out here, will you?"

"As soon as I figure out where 'here' is, I'll do just that! Come on, Linc."

The collie darted on ahead, moving quietly through the grass. They were in a flowery meadow, filled with blossoms that were yellow, blue, and deep red. Ari thought she recognized a few of the species. That was comforting. Surely that green and purplish-brown bloom in the shade of the trees was Jack-in-the-pulpit.

On the other hand, the little town on the other side of the field was not familiar at all. And that was not so comforting.

The village looked strange. For a moment, Ari wondered if Lori was right. Maybe they *had* been abducted by aliens. A wide dirt path ran straight down the middle of it. It was hard to tell at this distance, but the path appeared to end at a long, low, rambling structure made of wood that was too big for a house. Ari could make out a sign on a post in front of a big front porch. Maybe it was a hotel.

The left side of the path was lined with three-sided sheds. Some were big, some were small, but all contained many kinds of items. One shed had a spinning wheel out front. The shelves inside held brightly colored piles of yarnlike stuff. Several of the sheds had fenced paddocks attached. One of them held a few milk cows; another goats. And there was a bread shed, a fruit shed, a vegetable shed.

Houses — at least Ari guessed they were

houses — clustered on the opposite side of the dirt path like bees in a hive. The huts were round, with straw roofs. Most of them had bricklike chimneys. It was a warm morning, but smoke rose from a few of the huts and Ari guessed that the people here used wood fires to cook.

There were people in the village. That was a plus. And there was the smell of vegetable stew and melting cheese and freshly baked bread. That was a double plus.

But the women were dressed in long flowing gowns. . . .

Ari's mouth dropped open. Just like the dinner plates in Ann's kitchen!

And the men wore boots, tights, and loose shirts that looked as if they were made out of rough cotton. Some had short cloaks that were attached at the shoulder and fell to the waist. Ari had never seen clothes just like this before, or houses and shops and hotels.

"What is this place?" Lori said crossly. She shifted irritably on Chase's back. "What a dump! Where's the police station? This doesn't look right."

"I think it's because there are no power lines," Ari said. She realized she'd been clutching Linc's ruff. "No telephone poles, nothing like that."

"No cars, either. How do these people get around?" Lori gave a scornful sniff.

Shank's mare, Chase said. At Ari's puzzled look, *It's an expression we horses use for the way*

16

men walk. With two legs and those silly shoes you wear. I have no idea how your shoes stay on without nails, milady.

Ari didn't know quite what to say to this. She didn't know what she should do, either. Just walk down the dirt path and say, "Hi"? She and Lori were both dressed in denim shirts, breeches, and boots, so they didn't look as out of place as they might have. Jeans, T-shirts, and sneakers would have been very noticeable.

"So what do we do now?" Lori complained. She glared at Ari, pouting.

Chase looked at her with his wise brown eyes and breathed out softly.

Lincoln settled down on his haunches, scratched furiously at one ear, then looked at her expectantly.

Ari looked back at the three of them. *She* was supposed to decide?

"Well." Ari twirled a strand of hair with one finger. Then she twirled a strand of hair with the other. She squinted her eyes and tried to look thoughtful. Like a leader. She folded her arms across her chest and gazed sternly at the village.

What should they do? Just walk in?

The noise from the village was what you'd expect. People talking and laughing. Somebody was hammering metal somewhere, and the clangs split the air. One of the milk cows mooed in a thoughtful way while a woman in a long brown skirt with a shawl over her shoulders milked it. There was a jingling noise underneath all of this. It sounded just like the harness Ari used at Glacier River Farm when she hooked the pony to the cart. The jingling came from the woods to their left. Ari turned around as the sound grew louder.

"Morning! Morning, ladies!" A man driving a horse and a four-wheeled wagon waved to them as they trotted past. Except the horse wasn't really a horse.

It was a unicorn! A stout, black-and-white spotted unicorn, with a short black-and-white spiral horn coming straight out of the middle of his forehead! His harness was made of scarlet leather and his eyes were hazel. They widened at the sight of two girls, a collie, and a bronze stallion standing at the edge of the wood. He stopped and nodded to them.

The man driving the wagon jiggled the reins. "Move on, Toby. We're late — I say we're late with these vegetables." The man was very fat, with a smiling red face and a huge, curled mustache. He wore black loose-fitting trousers tucked into the top of heavy brown boots. His dark brown shirt was loose, too, but not loose enough to hide his enormous tummy.

"Hold on a minute, Samlett," the unicorn said in a very bossy way. Then, in the rudest voice Ari had ever heard, "And who, may I ask, are you?"

Lori shrieked. It was a faint shriek, mostly because she was too scared to get much breath into her lungs, but it was a shriek.

Toby scowled. "You are addressing a unicorn," he said loftily. "And that's how you pay your respects? By yelling?"

"It's talking," Lori gasped. She closed her eyes for a second. Her face was whiter than ever. "Oh, my. Oh, my. It's talking. It's a unicorn and it's talking. I want to go home."

"Well, Toby *does* talk a bit rude," Mr. Samlett admitted. "Hasn't been with me long, so there's not too much I can do about the way he talks, milady." He chewed one end of his mustache. "Rude to the others, too. And uppity. But there you are. It's like they say. Unicorns will be unicorns."

"I don't mean the way he's talking! I mean the fact that he's talking at all!" She threw Ari a poisonous glance. "I suppose *you* think it's perfectly normal."

"Now, your maid doesn't think a thing you don't want her to think," Mr. Samlett said nervously. "Don't get in an uproar, milady. Too fine a morning for that."

"Maid?" Ari said. "You think I'm her maid?"

"Well," Mr. Samlett said, "stands to reason, don't it? I mean, don't it? She's ridin' as fine a unicorn as I've ever seen in these parts, and you're doin' the walkin'." He leaned forward, squinting at

Chase. "Except, by gum. I say by gum. He don't have no horn, Toby."

"No, he doesn't," Toby said. He had a very odd expression in his eyes as he looked at Chase. Respect? Fear? Pity? Toby shook himself hard, as if to clear his brain. Then, resuming his former manner, he said, "Any fool could see that, except maybe you, Samlett."

"He's a horse," Ari said. "Not a unicorn."

"Looks like a unicorn to me," Mr. Samlett said. "Only he's got no horn. What happened to your horn, friend? If you don't mind my askin'."

Chase nudged Ari with his nose. *Say nothing for the moment, little one. We don't know how horses are treated in this place. And I — I cannot remember.*

"He doesn't talk," Lori said. "And you're both idiots. You heard her, he's a horse."

"Whatever you say, milady." Mr. Samlett rolled his eyes. "S'pose if he don't have a horn, he don't talk, neither. Didn't used to hear of such things. Not in Balinor. All the animals talk in Balinor. But the troubles are here, sure as you know it. More and more you hear of animals losin' their speech. Next thing you know, humans won't be able to talk, either. I say we won't be able to talk, either."

Ari bit her lip to keep from laughing. It might be a mercy if Mr. Samlett couldn't talk. But it was very sad about the animals.

He gave his mustache a final tug and asked Lori, "You and your maid headed into Balinor?"

20

"I'm not . . ." Ari began. Chase nudged her warningly. Toby, to everyone's amazement, began to laugh. When unicorns laugh (or, as Ari discovered later, sneeze, cough, hum, sing, or cry), they laugh through their horns.

"Now what stickerburr's under your saddle?" Mr. Samlett asked the unicorn genially.

"If there were a stickerburr under my saddle, do you think I would have agreed to pull this rickety old cart?" Toby demanded. "I would not. Why I'm laughing, I'll keep to myself for the moment. Ask this — lady — and her 'maid' and her dog and her hornless unicorn to come along to the Inn for breakfast."

"Ain't he something," Mr. Samlett said admiringly. "Never met a fellow with such a way with words. Well, how about it, milady?"

"Who, me?" Lori said. "I mean, yes. I want breakfast." She lifted her chin in the air and said in a highly snobbish way, "Breakfast for me and my maid. And a bath."

Lincoln growled under his breath, then tapped Ari's boot with his paw. She glanced down at him.

No baths!

Ari laughed and rumpled his ears. So Balinor, as Mr. Samlett called it, may be a different place, and they were in a different world, but some things were always the same.

3

They all rode down the dirt path through the village. Toby led the way, trotting briskly along while Mr. Samlett jounced in the cart. Once in a while, he would say, "Whoa, there, Toby." This had no effect whatsoever on the unicorn's speed, of course.

Lori rode behind the wagon on Chase. Chase held his head high, his neck arched. His silky mane flowed down his withers almost to his knees. His chestnut coat glimmered in the bright sunshine. Lincoln pranced along at his side.

Ari walked behind them all. She could see the torn spot in the back of Lori's breeches, but the flowered underwear was only visible when Lori tried to show off by posting bareback on Chase. Because she wasn't a very good rider — and because with all their adventures, everyone was tired — she posted once or twice, then gave it up. But she sat in a very lordly way, which made Ari chuckle to herself.

Mr. Samlett knew everyone in Balinor. Crutch, the Weaver, and his wife, Begonia. The vegetable man, the fruit girl with oranges, lemons, and peaches for sale. Even the milk cow, Falfa, said "Happy good morning" as they all went by.

Mr. Samlett said, "You should have heard the cow talk last week. The troubles have fallen on Balinor, sure enough. Something," Mr. Samlett continued, "has to be done."

Toby headed straight for the long, low wooden building at the end of the street, as Ari thought he would. The unicorn veered to the right as they approached the building. They passed the post with a sign hanging from it. Under the carving of a noble white unicorn with gold mane and horn, Ari read:

THE UNICORN INN

FINE FOOD, GOOD BEDS, STABLES

SAMLETT

The Inn was surrounded by flower gardens on three sides. Toby drew the wagon to the rear of the building. Here the yard was paved with worn red brick. There were stables on two sides with stalls that were much the same design as those at Glacier River Farm, with an upper and lower door. The upper doors were all open to the sunshine. There was an area for parking carts, wagons, and buggies on the third side of the yard. A large watering trough ran down the middle of the brick. Toby stopped in front of the trough, lowered his head, and drank some water.

Mr. Samlett heaved himself out of the wagon and gave a sharp whistle. Three or four heads poked out of the open stall doors.

Ari drew her breath. They were all unicorns. One was fine-boned, elegant, and satiny black. The nameplate on her stall door read BRYANNA. Her horn was solid ivory. A sapphire jewel glittered at the base of her horn, just where it met her forehead. The unicorn in the stall next to her looked very similar to the Belgian draft horses Ari knew at home. He was big, muscular, and solid, with a curly brown beard under his chin to match his curly brown mane.

Ari couldn't see much of the third unicorn, who shifted slightly in the dimness of her stall. But she had an impression of cool, violet grace and a silver mane. And she knew — she couldn't say why — that the unicorn inside was a mare.

"Bother. I say bother." Mr. Samlett looked as mournful as a man with a cheery red face could look. He whistled again. "Where is that dratted stable boy?"

"Gone to his mother's house for his name day," Toby said. "He told you that this morning, you boneheaded bozo. But did you listen? No. And do we have more guests with no human to care for them? Yes." He gave a derisive "blaat!" from his horn. "Now what are you going to do?"

"Why, I'll muck out and water them myself. I say myself." Mr. Samlett rubbed his chin. Then he tugged at his mustache. Ari noticed that he tugged at his mustache often. Maybe it helped him think. "Trouble is, I got lunch to make, and floors to sweep, and beds to see to. Here! I got an idea." He walked over to Chase and looked up at Lori. "How were you goin' to pay, milady?"

"Pay?" Lori gazed down at him, her eyebrows lifted in nervous astonishment. "Why, by credit card, of course." She drew her eyebrows together in an alarmed way. "That is . . ." She patted her breeches pocket. "If I brought it . . . oh!" She felt the tear in her breeches. "Oh, no! My pants are torn!"

"The maid will fix 'em for you," Mr. Samlett said. "Don't worry about that. Thing you want to worry about is how are you going to pay me? For the breakfast. Yes, the breakfast."

Lori pulled her father's credit card from her breeches pocket. She waved it at Mr. Samlett. "With this. I assume you take Visa?"

Mr. Samlett didn't look as happy as he had before. "I don't know a thing about this, milady. Not a thing. Now, you tell me what your house is, who your papa is, and maybe I can send him the bill. But the thing is, if that's all you got for money — why, it isn't. Money that is. Not in Balinor."

"This is money everywhere," Lori said loftily. "Check with the bank."

"With the bank? Why'n the name of Numinor himself would I want to go the riverbank? I say the riverbank?"

Toby cleared his horn with a loud "blaaat!"

This made everyone jump. But it got their attention. "Do you have any way to pay for your room at the Inn?"

"My fa —" Lori stopped herself, then bit her lip.

"Her father!" Mr. Samlett said. "And who might your father be, milady? Are you one of Lord Benterman's kin, perhaps? From the House of the Wheelwrights?" He jerked his thumb at Chase. "That unicorn . . ."

"Horse," Ari corrected him.

". . . is such a fine specimen even without his horn that you must be related to the Lords of the Roadways. I say the Roadways."

"We can't pay you," Ari said. "But we would be grateful if you would give us shelter for the night."

"Well now, well now." Mr. Samlett rubbed his hands together. "If you sold me that fine uni —"

"*Horse*," Ari said firmly. "And he's not for sale, Mr. Samlett. But if you don't have a stable boy, we can work for our food and shelter."

"Work?" Lori said. "Don't be ridiculous."

"Of course *you* won't have to lift a finger, milady. I say a finger. But your maid here looks like a fine strong girl, and I do need a stable hand." Mr. Samlett beamed. "How lucky we found one another! I need a stable hand, and your mistress needs a soft bed and a warm fire, for it will be cold tonight. And it all works out for the best. I say the best. You, girl . . ."

"Ari," Ari said, as firmly as she had said "horse."

"Ari!" he said with what he obviously thought was an amazing amount of generosity. "You can sleep in the grain room. There's a nice lot of old sacks in there, should keep you and the dog pretty warm. I say pretty warm."

"And Chase?" Ari asked. "May I work to put him in one of the empty stalls?"

"A hornless unicorn? And one that doesn't talk? My goodness no, my girl. He can stay with the milk cow in the village, or in the field out back. I say out back. He'll get plenty to eat, never you fear."

So Ari — with kind but firm instructions from Mr. Samlett — set about earning their meals and a place to sleep.

Mr. Samlett insisted that Lori go to her room, take a hot bath, and eat a meal. Ari, he said, could begin her stable duties right away and join them all in the Inn for supper.

With Lincoln at her side, Ari put Chase in one of the small paddocks near the stable yard and made sure that he had water. Mr. Samlett showed her where the hay was stacked. It was beautiful hay, thick, properly green, that looked so delicious Ari could have eaten some herself. She hauled two large flakes out to the stallion and dropped them in front of him.

"I don't know about this hay, Chase," she said.

27

"I probably shouldn't give you too much. What if you get colic on this strange food?"

Chase turned it over with his nose. *It smells like summer, milady. I will be careful how much I eat. But it is beautiful.*

"You'll be all right while I go to work?"

He dropped his muzzle in her hair and breathed out twice. This meant he was contented, so Ari and her dog went back to the stable yard. There she found out what a help it was being able to talk to Lincoln. He fetched her the broom, so she could sweep the brick yard, and carried the water buckets when she emptied the watering trough and cleaned it.

When the sun was straight overhead, a bell clanged. Mr. Samlett came out of the Inn, carrying a wooden bowl of delicious vegetable stew, a hunk of mild cheese, and bread. Ari sat on an overturned bucket and shared her meal with Linc. The unicorns in the stalls had pushed open their stall doors (there were no latches or locks) and gone for a stroll in the market. All except the one who lurked in violet and silver shadows, who had no name on her door. Ari could see the tip of her crystal horn glinting in the sunlight, but nothing else. She swallowed her last spoonful of stew, rinsed her bowl in the trough, then walked to the stall.

"Hello?" she said tentatively.

There was no answer. Just a slight shifting in

the lavender shadow and a stir in the fragrant air. Ari peeked in.

The most beautiful unicorn was asleep in the straw! She was the color of the sky just as the sun goes down, a murmur of lavender, violet, and blue. Her cheek lay on a silk pillow. Her delicate legs were folded under her belly. Her silvery mane rippled over her back and touched the fresh sweet straw on the floor. But it was the horn that drew Ari's fascinated gaze. It was long and translucent, twisted like a seashell. A diamond gleamed at the base.

Ari held her breath. The stall was magnificent. A silver-bordered mirror was hung on one wall while an ornate silver bridle and silver velvet saddle hung on racks on another. There was even a silver manure bucket tucked neatly in the corner. "Wow!" Ari said softly.

Linc reared up and put his front paws on the edge of the stall door. At the sight of the unicorn, his ears went up. There was an eager, adoring look in his eye. He dropped to the ground outside the door in a crouch. Ari bent down and ran her hands over his silken head.

"Are you okay, Linc?" she whispered.

It is the Lady! The Dreamspeaker of the Celestial Valley! He closed his eyes. *And I have seen her! I am the luckiest of dogs!*

"Well," Ari said in a low voice, so as not to wake the unicorn from her nap, "why doesn't the luckiest of dogs help me with the manure buckets? There's a lot to do to tidy up before those other unicorns come back. And Mr. Samlett said they like their stalls cleaned before the evening meal. So let's get cracking!"

All the buckets were emptied, the straw raked and turned over, the mirrors in each unicorn's stall polished until they shone. Ari left the violet unicorn's stall for last, to give her the maximum time to sleep. But when she tapped timidly at the stall door, she discovered the lovely being had gone out, perhaps to join the others, perhaps to wander by herself in the woods.

Finally, with the sun just touching the edge of the western horizon, Ari's work was finished.

Mr. Samlett came bustling out of the Inn door. "This is just a fine job, a fine job," he beamed. "Now, come in a bit before the dinner hour, will you? You will want to wash and change, I expect. And my good wife found you a proper kirtle."

"Sir?" Ari asked, bewildered.

"Ah, I forgot. Your mistress said you were from the north." He shook his head. "Strange customs they have up north, up north. And you lost your luggage in that stream, besides. We will give you something to wear, instead of those boys' clothes you had to borrow. But you must come and see your mistress now. She desires your presence."

"She does, huh?" Ari said a little grimly. It was just as well that good old Lori had "desired her presence." They'd better get their stories straight about who they were and where they came from. Although she had to admire the fib about losing their clothes in the stream, whatever stream that may have been. None of the women or girls she'd seen in Balinor wore breeches.

Ari had thought quite a lot about their predicament while she had been sweeping, stacking, washing, and mucking out. Someone in Balinor had to know about the Gap, and how to get back to Glacier River. But she needed time to figure out who to ask. She had seen that Balinor had its bad side, just like the dangerous parts of cities near Glacier River Farm. Those red-eyed unicorns had been terrifying. And then there were these mysterious troubles, with animals losing their ability to talk. She wanted to find out a lot more about this place before she went around telling people they were from another world. And if Mr. Samlett gave them clothes to help them look more like the people who lived here — it'd be a great help. They'd be in disguise.

"Well, girl?" Mr. Samlett demanded.

"I'm sorry, I was thinking of something else," she explained. "Thanks very much for the loan of the clothes, and yes, I would like a bath. And sure, I'll go see that bra . . . I mean, Mistress Lori now."

Ari liked the inside of the Inn right away. The whole place was made of solid wood — wood floors, wood tables and benches, wood walls. A wide flight of stairs in the middle of the room led to the second floor. A huge stone fireplace took up the entire south wall. There were several people sitting around the big room, all of them adults. Ari kept Linc close by her side.

"You go right up them stairs and turn right. Your mistress's room is number twelve. My good wife gave her your new clothes. And the bath is just down the hall."

Ari ran lightly up the stairs, Lincoln clicking along behind. She tapped at door number 12 and pushed it open.

"Oh," Lori said, "it's you." She sat on a bench in front of a small fireplace.

The room was small, with a low ceiling, a small window, a huge bed, and a chest against one wall. Lori had changed her torn breeches and shirt for a long blue dress that buttoned all the way to a high neck. Her riding boots — scratched and muddy — lay in a tangle of clothes on the floor. "You can pick those up and polish them." She pointed to her boots.

"You wish." Ari sat down on the bed. She was tired.

"Well? You're my maid, aren't you?"

"Forget it, Lori. I'm in no mood. And it wouldn't hurt for you to help with the chores."

"What? A lady like me? No way. It'd shock them out of their little leather sandals." She stood up and roamed around the room. She bit her lower lip. "Have you figured a way out of this mess?"

"Not yet. But I will. What kind of story did you tell Mr. Samlett?"

"That we were traveling from up north and some bears scared us and we lost our luggage in a stream."

"Bears? What if there aren't any bears here!"

"You told me there were bears here. And Samlett didn't know what I meant until I told him about the sound of the marching." She shuddered.

"What did he say then?"

Lori's voice was so low, Ari could hardly hear her. "There are things that walk these woods. Terrible things. And we are not to go out at night." She shivered. "I believe him, too. I'm not setting foot out of this place until you figure out a way to get us out of here."

"Did Mr. Samlett's wife leave some clothes for me?"

Lori pointed to the chest. "In there."

"And the bathroom?"

"Bathroom! Ha!" Lori's laugh was scornful. "You call a big bucket and a little bucket a bathroom?"

"A big bucket and a little bucket?"

"One to wash in and one to . . . you know. Anyhow, take a left in the hall when you leave. And you can leave anytime soon."

Ari, who had opened the chest and was examining the contents, said in an absentminded way, "I'll take this skirt and this jacket. I'm going to leave my boots on. Then I'll go downstairs and hang out. See if I can find anyone to talk to."

"Fine," Lori snapped. "Just fine. Leave me here all by myself. I've been by myself all day."

"Oh, for goodness' sake. Look, Linc will keep you company while I wash up. And then we'll go downstairs together, okay?"

Lori gave a pitiful sniff. She had her usual mean expression, but there were big tears in her eyes. Ari sighed. "It's going to be fine."

"It is NOT going to be fine! What if we never get home?"

Ari folded the skirt and jacket in her arms. "Don't you worry. We'll get back. I know we will."

"I'm not moving out of this room until I find out we're going home."

Ari rolled her eyes, left the room, and stood in the hall. The very air here smelled different from the air at the farm. Wood torches burned in holders on the walls, so even the light was different.

Would they ever get back to the farm? Ari rubbed her face with her hands. She was tired. So tired.

She bit her lip. The thought was strong in her, strangely persistent.

She didn't want to go back. Not yet. Not yet.

There was something about this place that called to her heart.

4

Lincoln waited patiently outside the wash-room while Ari bathed and changed. The dark red skirt had pretty embroidery around the hem but was a little big around the middle, so she rolled up the waistband. The blouse was made of a soft, off-white cotton and had full sleeves and a scoop neck that tied with two strings. The leather vest fit snugly and it would be nice and warm as the evening cooled. She wound her hair up on top of her head and clipped it with her barrettes. The only real problem were her riding boots. Her socks were filthy after the long day of adventure, but there was no way she would wear her boots without socks. So she pulled her socks on and her boots and opened the door.

She was ready.

Lincoln was lying on the floor, cleaning his

little white forepaws. When she came out, he jumped to his feet and met her, head low, tail wagging. *You look like one of them!*

"Is that good or bad, Linc?" She sighed. "Are *they* good or bad?"

If they are bad, his thought was fierce, *I will bite them and bite them!*

"Thanks. I think."

She paused at the top of the stairs. The room was lit by torches. A big log burned in the fireplace. The great wooden door to the outside opened and closed as people came in. A draft of cold air drifted up the stairs and Ari shivered. She was glad she had on the leather vest. It was cool here in Balinor, once the sun set.

The room was filled with townspeople. Some drank from wooden cups, others ate bread, cheese, and peaches. Could she slip among them, unnoticed? Would they talk in front of her, a stranger? They all seemed to know one another.

She surveyed the room. Bread, cheese, peaches. Of course! She could walk around with a wooden tray and pretend to be a waitress. Nobody really paid too much attention to waitresses.

She ran lightly down the stairs and took a platter of peaches from the sideboard near the kitchen door. Then she watched the group of jabbering people carefully. A tall man with gray hair stood talking in the very center of the room. His clothes were expensive: Soft leather boots came to his knees and the short cloak over his shoulders was trimmed with pearls. His hair was gray and he had a neatly trimmed beard. The men around him seemed to be listening carefully to what he was saying. A woman stood there, too. She was tall and slim with dark hair and black eyes. Her face was smooth. Ari had never seen such a perfectly white complexion. Dark jewels winked in her hair. She and the man looked like important people from the way they dressed and acted. It would be smart to start with them, Ari thought.

Ari edged her way through the crowd, offering the tray of peaches with a smile. She stopped right in back of the man with the pearl cloak, then picked over the peaches with a frown. "Oh, my," she said, to no one in particular, "several of these have brown spots." She picked up peaches, examined them, then set them down again.

All the while she was listening.

"The Shifter's forces grow bolder every day," the tall man said. His voice was low, but urgent. "I had word the Demon herd moved through the King's forest today. In broad daylight."

"Aye, I heard that as well," the woman said. Her voice was quiet and distinguished. "But you should not call it the King's forest, milord Lexan. Not even here at the Unicorn Inn, where we think we are safe. It's the Shifter's forest now."

"But we are the King's men here," said another man.

"And the Queen's," the woman responded. "Wherever they may be."

"May the One Who Rules us all bless them both." That was Mr. Samlett. Ari tucked her chin down and turned the peaches over and over. The Innkeeper sounded anxious as he asked, "There's been no word? No word at all of where the cursed Shifter has hidden them?"

"They remain hostage. No one knows where." That was Lord Lexan again. "Our only hope is the Princess herself. I tell you again, we must beg her to come from the safe place, to lead us against the Shifter and his devil army."

"She's only a girl, my brother," Lady Kylie said. "About the age of my own daughter. I would not put a mere girl in danger. That is why the Resistence appealed to Numinor to send her away."

"And because of who she is, we must bring her back again! I tell you, that lying usurper has broken every oath he gave after he stole the throne! All would remain as it had when the King and Queen ruled," Lord Lexan said. "There would be no reason to fight. The only difference would be that *he* would ride the Lord of the Unicorns at Midsummer. That only *he* would place the Crown of Balinor upon his head. And look how long he kept his word — a mere three months! And now what is happening? The Shifter's men stormed my manor not three days past! They ravaged my crops, stole my hay and corn, burned my barns. And the unicorns. The unicorns' language is disappearing. Without their language, we will not be able to speak with the animals who live in the forests and on our farms. Already the animals of our kingdom are losing the ability to speak. The Lord of the Unicorns has disappeared. His mistress, the Princess, is in hiding. I tell you, we must bring her back. We must ride against the Shifter!"

The crowd murmured in agreement. Lincoln pressed his head against Ari's knee. *Just our luck. We arrive right in the middle of a war.*

"It seems a lot more important than our being lost," Ari said to him. "And it's sad about the animals. The unicorns especially."

I don't know what we can do about it. Lincoln yawned. *I'm tired.*

"It might be better to see what we can find out in the morning," Ari agreed.

"Peach, girl?"

Ari looked up. The man in the pearl-encrusted cloak was smiling at her. Lord Lexan, they had called that woman's brother. "May I have a peach?" he asked Ari.

"Why, yes, sir. Of course, sir." Ari offered him the tray. Lord Lexan narrowed his gray eyes at her. "You aren't from Balinor. I don't believe I've seen you before."

"Um, no, sir. I'm from up north. We just arrived today."

"North? That's Arlen's territory. The Lord of the Six Seas. Are you from his House?"

From the way he said "House," Ari was pretty sure he didn't mean a little hut with a straw roof. He meant a castle — or at least a mansion. He looked kind, and he looked as if he might know a bit more about this world than Mr. Samlett. She took a deep breath and said recklessly, "Well, sir, my friends and I. We're from north of the Gap."

The room went still as a graveyard. Everyone stared at her. Lincoln growled.

Ari was scared, but determined not to show it. She stuck her chin up a little. "Do you know the Gap, sir? Actually, my friends and I would like to go home, except we don't seem to be able to . . . to . . . find . . ." She stopped talking. Lord Lexan's face was as grim as death.

"Samlett!" he snapped.

The crowd around Lord Lexan parted to reveal the Innkeeper. His chubby face was drawn tight with fear. "I didn't know, sir. I swear, I didn't know, sir."

Ari cleared her throat. She hoped her voice wouldn't shake. "Is there something wrong with the Gap?"

"Wrong with the — ha!" Lord Lexan flung his head back and laughed. But it was not a happy laugh. It was definitely an angry laugh. "She is young to be a spy, is she not, Samlett?"

Mr. Samlett's normally red face was pale. "You know, girl, surely you must know. The Shifter is from beyond the Gap."

"Oh," Ari said. "Um, no, I didn't know. Who is the Shifter?"

"She claims not to know? Ha!" The woman whose voice had seemed so kind pushed her way past Mr. Samlett and grabbed Ari's chin with one ringed hand. She tilted it up so that the flickering torch light fell on it. "She looks innocent. More than innocent. She has a look of the Royal family itself. This is the Shifter's work, I swear. It is well known that he can take any shape. Any form. That he moves among us unannounced, to spy and do his filthy work of destruction. I say we lock her up. We lock her up and let justice deal with her!"

5

"That's a bit fierce, my dear. All over a mere girl?" Lord Lexan put his hand on the angry woman's back. "I don't think the young girl quite understands what she's saying, Kylie."

"She doesn't look like a simpleton to me," the Lady Kylie snapped. "Far from it."

"Thanks, I think," Ari muttered. Which was worse? To have people think she was an idiot or to be locked up? It seemed safer to be an idiot. She dropped her mouth open, to look as stupid as possible. "Peaches, milady? I — oops!" She tilted the tray and the peaches spilled all over the floor. A particularly ripe one rolled against Lady Kylie's velvet shoe and splattered. The people nearest Ari backed up. A few of them bent down and began to pick up the peaches. Ari kicked the ripe peach away from the outraged Kylie, then she stepped on it. Ripe peach squished all over the floor.

"Clumsy fool!" Lady Kylie hissed.

"Now then, now then!" Mr. Samlett wiped his perspiring face with a large red cloth. "And such a good stable hand, too! Nobody cleans stalls like this one, milady."

"Then confine her to the stables! And keep her out of the way of the gentry!" Lady Kylie's smooth face was drawn tight with irritation.

"Sorry, milady," Ari said. She pretended to sniff. Then she wiped her nose with her sleeve. Lady Kylie made a disgusted noise.

Mr. Samlett made shooing motions. "Isn't there work for you with your mistress, girl?"

"Why don't I check on the unicorns, sir?" Ari suggested. She wanted out of this room. There were things she had to discuss with Chase.

"Fine. Fine! Just don't smear them with ripe peaches. I say ripe peaches. Especially the unicorn with the crystal horn. You must take great care around her, girl!"

"Crystal horn?" Lady Kylie said sharply. She narrowed her eyes. "And who might that be, Samlett?"

"Oh, a very beautiful unicorn, milady. Very beautiful. My cart unicorn Toby made the arrangements for her lodging. He is working to pay for her room and board. I haven't actually met her, of course," he added in a bewildered way. "She never seems to be in her stall when I go to see if the arrangements are satisfactory. But I've seen the crystal horn and the jewel on it."

43

"A unicorn with a servant?" Lady Kylie sneered. "I've never heard of such a thing. And Balinor unicorns don't have precious jewels on their horns. Just those of the Royal court. And they all disappeared when the King and Queen did."

"The unicorns who live in the Celestial Valley have jewels on their horns," someone at the back of the crowd said.

"Legends!" Lady Kylie scoffed. "Mere legends."

"Oh, no, milady," Samlett said earnestly. "Why, you don't believe in Numinor and the Rainbow herd?"

"I believe in what I see," Lady Kylie snapped. "And if our unicorns need to believe in gods and goddesses that don't exist, that's fine with me. But I have seen the Royal unicorns, Samlett, when milord Lexan and I attended the King and Queen at court. Before the troubles began. And if there's a Royal unicorn in your stable, man, she should not be here at this Inn!"

"That's true," Lord Lexan said with a slightly puzzled air. "If she is one of the Royals. Could it be, Samlett? Do you have a Royal unicorn at your Inn?"

"I didn't dare ask!" Mr. Samlett said.

"We will ask her now!" Lady Kylie said. "I've never heard of such a thing! A Royal housed in *your* Inn, Samlett. It's ridiculous."

"It's a very fine Inn, milady," Mr. Samlett protested.

44

"Take me to her at once!" Lady Kylie stamped her foot. A bit of peach flew up in the air. "If what you say is true, I shall invite her to our manor house. Where she will be in company fit for her, Samlett!"

Ari was amused to see that Mr. Samlett could walk backward and bow at the same time. He backed and bowed across the stable yard, apologizing to Lady Kylie and Lord Lexan all the way. Ari followed them, keeping well back so that Lady Kylie wouldn't notice her. Lincoln pattered unobtrusively behind them all.

But when they reached the stall, the beautiful unicorn was gone.

"She was right here, milady!" Mr. Samlett protested. "The light from the torches isn't very good. Maybe she's in the back. I say in the back of the stall."

But the violet unicorn wasn't there. The silver bridle was gone from the wall. All that remained was the scent of flowers.

"You've been drinking too much of your own punch, Samlett!" Lord Lexan said.

"I didn't believe him for a minute!" Lady Kylie sniffed. "A Royal unicorn here!"

"These are strange times," Lord Lexan observed. "Come, my dear. It's late. We should be heading back to our home. Samlett, ask our unicorns if they are ready to be hitched to our carriage."

"If they will hear me, milord," Samlett said apologetically. "I'm afraid that when I turned them out to pasture this morning, I say turned them out, they spoke very little to me."

"Outrageous!" Lady Kylie said. "Our unicorns losing their ability to speak? They wouldn't dare!"

If she were a unicorn of Lady Kylie's, she wouldn't speak to that horrible woman, either, Ari thought. Then she volunteered, "Shall I go ask them, Mr. Samlett? It's the pair of matched chestnuts in stalls three and four, isn't it?"

"You go ask them, girl. I say ask them. And then hitch them up, if you would."

"It's Ari," she reminded him firmly.

Lady Kylie gave her a suspicious glance. Ari slipped out of the stall before Lady Kylie could question her further. She and Linc walked down the brick path to stalls three and four. Lord Lexan's unicorns were both there, dozing peacefully. Ari looked at the first over the half door, which was open to the fresh night air. His name was written on a piece of slate attached to the lower door — NATHAN. She suddenly felt shy. It seemed so odd to be talking to unicorns!

"Excuse me," she said tentatively. "Hello? Nathan?"

Nathan jerked his head up, startled out of sleep. He nodded at her. He was short and powerfully built, with well-muscled hindquarters and sturdy legs.

"I'm Ari, the um . . . stable hand. Lord Lexan asked if you were ready to draw the carriage home."

46

"Home," Nathan said in a confused way. His voice sounded rusty, as if it hadn't been used for a while.

"Shall I hitch you and . . ." She ducked her head to take a look at the nameplate on stall three. "And Orrin up to the carriage?"

"Orrin," Nathan said more clearly.

"Nathan?" Orrin stuck his head out of his stall. He looked exactly like Nathan. Ari wondered if they were brothers.

The carriage harness was hung on Orrin's wall. Ari took both unicorns into the courtyard and backed them into the carriage shafts. Then she hitched up the harness. Both unicorns stood placidly and did whatever she asked.

"What are you doing? I say what are you doing?"

Ari jumped. She didn't hear Mr. Samlett come up behind her. "Hitching the unicorns up," she said. She wanted to add, "Isn't it obvious?" but didn't.

"But *you* are guiding them!" Mr. Samlett said. "It's as if they don't know what you want them to do! Oh, dear! I say oh, dear! I wonder if Lord Lexan will be able to get home!"

"They're very well-trained unicorns," Ari offered. "I'm sure all he has to do is use the reins."

"Use the reins? I say use the reins!"

"That's how you communicate with a ho . . . I mean, a unicorn. Isn't it?"

47

"Not in Balinor," Mr. Samlett said. "No, not in Balinor. And where did you say you were from again?" Ari waved her hand vaguely in the air. "Up North?"

Ari stayed well out of the way when Lord Lexan and Lady Kylie got into the carriage. It was a bit of a comedy. Lord Lexan took up the reins and said, "Home, Nathan and Orrin."

Both unicorns just stood there. It looked as if Nathan had fallen back asleep.

"We said *home!*" Lady Kylie said sharply.

Nothing happened.

"Cluck," Ari suggested.

"What!" Lady Kylie glared at her.

"Go like this." Ari made a clucking noise. Both Nathan and Orrin jerked their heads up at the sound. "And then flex the reins like this." Ari shook her hands into the air. Lord Lexan tried it. The unicorns moved off, slowly, in an erratic manner.

"Well, at least they are headed home," Mr. Samlett said woefully. "Hard times, my dear. I say hard times. How did you learn not to talk to unicorns and still get them to help you?"

"Um," Ari said. "Well, I ride quite a bit. At home."

"Of course. Your own unicorn cannot speak. So you must have learned these things."

"He's a horse," Ari corrected him firmly.

"Whatever you say. You must teach me how to do this," Mr. Samlett said. "If the troubles continue, we are all going to need to learn this unspoken language. I say all of us. Well, I'm for my bed, my dear. You gave me good help today. I say good help. If you want to leave that demanding mistress of yours, you'll always have a job here, I say always. I need someone like you. In times like these." He shook his head, sighed, and went back to the Inn.

Do we go to sleep now, too? Linc asked.

"Not yet, boy. I need to see to Chase."

You always think about Chase first! He looked up at her, eyes soft and pleading. *It's dangerous in this place. I can smell it. I can hear it. We should go back to the room where Lori is. It's safe there.*

Ari knelt down and ran her fingers around his ears. "I don't know that it's safe anywhere, Linc. And I have to see to Chase. He needs me."

I need you, too, Linc growled.

Ari laughed. "We need each other. All of us. And that includes Lori. Come on now, I need to find a currycomb, if they have currycombs in Balinor. I'll brush Chase and then I'll brush you."

Linc located a very nice currycomb with a wood back and soft wooden teeth. Ari collected a bucket of oats and a bucket of fresh water. They found Chase alert in his paddock, ears up, eyes facing the north.

"There's no moon tonight," Ari commented as she gently combed out his mane.

That isn't good, her stallion replied. He bent his head and breathed gently into her hair.

"Why not?"

Chase shifted restlessly on his feet. *I don't know. I think I knew once, but I've forgotten. As I've forgotten so many things. But there is danger when there is no moon.*

Ari commanded Chase to "stand," then went to work on his coat. After a moment he said, *There is magic here in Balinor.*

"I know. I wonder if that's why you can talk to me all the time now. But I wish you could talk out loud, Chase. And Linc, too. And there's another thing I wish. I'd like to meet that unicorn, the one with the crystal horn. But she's gone from her stall."

There is mystery here, Chase agreed. *And something bad is out there, milady. I can feel it.*

Ari straightened up and listened hard. The night was quiet. "I'd say the whole thing was a mystery." She shrugged her shoulders and yawned suddenly. She was tired, and she hurried to finish up.

She ran her hands down Chase's right foreleg, then tapped his ankle. Obediently, he lifted his hoof. She brushed the dirt and stones out as well as she could. She brushed out his other hooves in turn. She'd have to find a hoof pick. "If they have currycombs in Balinor, they must have hoof picks," Ari said cheerfully. "There. You're all set. I brought you some oats, and fresh water and . . ."

"ARI!" It was a woman's voice, high and commanding.

Lincoln jumped to his feet and growled. Ari

50

felt Chase come to full alert beside her. "Yes?" she called. "I'm over here!"

"Come back to the Inn! Now, if you please!"

"It's Lady Kylie," Ari said. "I suppose she's forgotten something. Or maybe the unicorns just turned around and wandered back here. Sleep well, Chase."

Ari! Don't go!

She looked up at him. There was a line of worry between his eyes. "Why not?"

He stamped the ground. *I don't know! By the moon, I don't know. If I could only remember!* He raised his head and whinnied, a long, angry call full of frustration.

"Hush!" Ari said. "You'll wake everyone up." She smoothed his forelock, her fingers tender over the white scar.

"Girl!" Lady Kylie shrieked. Ari looked over her shoulder. The Inn door was open, and Lady Kylie stood there, a dim figure against the light from inside. Her hands were on her hips.

"I'll be right there!" She gave Chase a final pat. "I'll see you in the morning. Come on, Linc." She climbed through the fence boards, Linc wriggling after her. She jogged toward the Inn, hoping that Lady Kylie and Lord Lexan hadn't decided to stay the night. She'd have to unharness the poor unicorns again, and she was really tired. Behind her, Chase let out another long, loud whinny.

"Yes?" Ari said as she came up to the angry woman.

"Come in here, please." Lady Kylie stepped aside. Ari walked into the room. A chill prickled the back of her neck, and she stopped. Linc pressed close to her side.

Something was wrong. There were people in the room, as there had been earlier in the evening. But those had been the townspeople of Balinor. These men and women looked the same — at first glance.

Maybe it was the air in the room that was confusing. Perhaps Mr. Samlett had placed a wet log on the fire by mistake, because the whole room was full of a sort of thin, oily smoke. Not smoke, exactly, but a brackish haze. It made it hard to see who these people were.

Ari squeezed her eyes shut and opened them again. Everyone except Lady Kylie was dressed in long cloaks. The hoods were drawn over their heads so that she couldn't tell the men from the women.

The fire blazed up suddenly, revealing the face of what Ari thought was a little boy beside the fireplace. Ari backed up. The short ones weren't children. They were very short adults with twisted faces.

"Where's Lord Lexan?" Ari asked. "Is . . . um . . . anything wrong?"

"Oh, yes, there's something wrong," Lady Kylie hissed. She moved closer. The fire blazed up again. The flames were reflected in her eyes.

Ari was suddenly very afraid. "Tell you what, milady," she said. "Maybe I'll just go up to my room. . . ." She edged backward toward the stairs.

"We know who you are." Lady Kylie opened her mouth to smile. Ari swallowed hard. The woman's teeth were sharp and pointed like a fox.

"Get her!" Lady Kylie commanded.

The cloaked figures gathered together slowly, like droplets of oil forming a pool. Lincoln barked, and barked again. Suddenly, the collie was a whirlwind, teeth bared, eyes hot and angry. He growled and bit, moving as fast as the wind.

The crowd fell back. Someone screamed.

Run, Ari! Run! Lincoln shouted.

"I won't leave you here!"

You must! A hand reached out to grab her. Its nails were long and pointed. Lincoln darted forward and sank his teeth into it. Blood flew around his jaws. *Go now! Go now! I cannot save us both!*

"I can't leave you!"

THEY DON'T WANT ME! THEY WANT YOU! RUN!

Ari picked up her skirts, ran for the back door, and pushed it open. Lincoln, a whirlwind of teeth and claws, kept the crowd at bay. She fell outside gasping. Thank goodness there were no latches here. She turned for a last look at her gallant collie. What she saw then would haunt her for the rest of her life. Lady Kylie came at the dog with a flaming torch. She whirled it once around her head, then brought it down with all her might onto Lincoln's silken head.

The collie yelped and fell like a stone to the floor.

The door swung closed in Ari's face.

Ari fought the urge to open the door and plunge into the crowd. "Keep calm, keep calm," she muttered to herself. If she went back in, she would be captured. And there would be no way at all to help Linc. But if she went for help . . . where was Mr. Samlett?

Ari pulled a heavy bench in front of the door. The crowd pounded against it. It wouldn't be long before they broke it open. She spun around. A hiding place! She had to find a hiding place!

Starlight shone on the brick yard, bleaching the ruddy bricks. The white light fell on the stable doors, closed now against the cool night air. The top of one door swung open. A low, sweet voice called out, "Arianna. Come here."

The door behind her bulged with the force of angry blows. The bench shifted out.

"Ari. You must come here. Now."

Ari ran. She flung herself over the bottom half of the stall door and fell into the straw. She landed on her leg, and bit her lip so she wouldn't scream. She heard the Inn door burst open with a terrible *cra-a-a-a-ck!* She picked herself up and peeked over the door. People poured into the yard.

A few carried torches snatched from the rough-hewn walls of the Inn. They swung the torches in a wide circle.

"She can't have gone far!" Lady Kylie shouted. "Check the stables!"

"Arianna. Lie down. I will cover you with the straw." The twilight-colored unicorn drifted toward her, as if she were dancing on air. "Come. Do as I say."

6

"But . . . how do you know my name?" she asked shyly. The Dreamspeaker, poor Linc had called her. She seemed like a goddess, encased in silvery light.

"Hurry."

Ari flung herself into the straw. The unicorn bent her lovely head. The crystal horn flashed as she used it to toss straw over Ari.

Someone thumped urgently on the unicorn's stall door.

"And who disturbs me?" the twilight-colored unicorn asked.

"Lady. We beg your pardon. But we seek a young girl. With hair the color of bronze, and eyes like the sky." Lady Kylie again. Ari wondered why she'd thought the woman sounded distinguished. There was something horrible about her voice. Something snakelike.

56

"And you seek her here? Go away. Do not disturb my rest."

There was a long pause. Then, "Lady. We must obey of course. Will you bless our search? She is a traitor, this one, and a spy."

"I bless all searches for traitors and spies. Now go. Leave me."

There was a respectful murmur from the crowd outside. Ari held her breath. There was a sound of many footsteps, marching away into the night. Ari let her breath out softly. Long moments went by, then the bell-like voice said, "You may come out now, Arianna."

"I'm not a traitor or a spy. I don't even know what's going on!"

"I understand. Come out."

Ari emerged from the straw. A pale light surrounded the unicorn, and although there were no lamps or torches, Ari could see her clearly. She stood near her mirror. To the girl's dazzled eyes, there seemed to be two violet unicorns before her.

"You left the ruby. On the other side."

Ari's hand went to her throat. "The necklace Lincoln brought me when I was in the hospital? Why . . . how did you know about that?"

"You shall see." The unicorn turned to the mirror. She arched her neck and blew out softly, twice. The mirror clouded over, then rippled, like water in a shallow stream. "I am Atalanta. As your friend the collie said, I am sometimes called the

57

Dreamspeaker. This is all I have of my Watching Pool," she added. "But it will do for now."

"But the Gap. If you know about my necklace and where I left it, you know about the Gap. Please, milady. Can you . . . Will you send me and my friends back?"

"Come and see."

Hesitantly, Ari looked into the mirror. She didn't see anything at first, just the still surface of the water. It was weird, looking into vertical water. The water rippled, as if a stone had been dropped into it. Ari gasped. She was looking at herself in her bedroom at Glacier River Farm! She watched as she took the ruby necklace from her neck and put it carefully into her dresser. Then, the vision in the mirror shifted to Dr. Bohnes's clinic, and the note she'd written on the window: SELL THE DOG LEASH!

"That was a mistake," the unicorn said. "Made with good heart, but a mistake nonetheless."

"Why?"

"Watch again." Atalanta breathed out once, sharply, as a mare does when calling a foal out of danger. The water rippled, darkened.

Ari drew back with a gasp. Unicorns with fiery eyes paraded through the forest. She shuddered. "Ugh. I saw them today. The Demon unicorns."

"The Shifter's work," Atalanta said sadly. "My herd mates, once upon a time. But that is not a story to tell you here and now." The coal-black horde of unicorns marched across the watery screen, a grim and terrible sight. The leader of the column whirled suddenly, then brought his head up, as if he knew he was being watched. He turned slowly, slowly. Ari shrank back. The unicorn's head, rimmed in fire, blacker than the depths of the deepest cave, filled the Watching Pool mirror and stared directly into Ari's face.

"I know that eye!" she gasped. "Oh, please, please! Take it away! Turn it off!"

Atalanta blew once on the water, a sharp explosion of breath. The evil vision vanished. "Yes, you know that Eye. That is Entia, or one of the forms that Entia takes. He is what was searching for you, in the meadow at Glacier River. That Eye, the Eye of the Shifter, is looking for you everywhere. He will stalk you, search for you until he finds you."

"But why?" Ari burst out. "Why me? I haven't done anything."

"It's not what you've done. It's who you are." The unicorn stepped closer, so close that her long mane, as light as dandelion seeds and as soft as rose petals, draped Ari in a magical veil.

"Do you not remember, Arianna?" She blew gently onto Ari's face, just as Chase did when he told Ari that he loved her.

The last six months tumbled through Ari's mind like gravel falling down a slope: the days before she learned Chase could talk to her, when she was just Ann and Frank's foster daughter, Dr. Bohnes's friend, Frank's best worker in the stable.

And then — some memories came back. They were erratic. Like fireflies winking off and on, on and out. But there were memories. Just enough. The days before Glacier River Farm.

The days when she had lived here, in Balinor.

"I'm that Princess they talked about," Ari said dully. "I remember some of it now. Oh, I remember now. There was no accident. There was no car wreck. The Shifter caught me. Caught my mother, the Queen. Hid her, kidnapped her, sent her away. Stole my father, the King. And he has gone from the Kingdom to the Caves beneath the Six Seas, where no one has gone before."

"Yes, my dearest dear." Atalanta's amethyst eyes were sad.

"And I . . . I am Arianna." She raised her head, a sudden hope flooding her. "My brothers? Tace and Bren?"

"The Princes were taken, too."

"Oh, no. Oh, no." Ari sank to her knees in the straw. She remembered now. She wished she hadn't. The Palace, with its reflecting pools and large gardens. The white stone terrace overlooking the sea. Her mother . . . no. Too painful, the memories now. That last day. The day of the Great Betrayal . . . the shouts and screams of terror. The Shifter himself, a

60

terrible shadow, grabbing her, flinging her through space.

She cried hot tears. "Why, you were there, milady. You took me through the Gap."

"We sent you, yes. With the help of the people of this village."

Ari was bewildered. "But why didn't they recognize me? I mean, if the people here are, as they said, the King's men. And they helped me and my family as best as they could. . . ."

"They've helped you more than you know."

"But why didn't they know who I was tonight!?"

"You have been gone from Balinor awhile, Arianna."

"Yes. Lord Lexan said that traitors could be among us, among my people, and we would never know it because the Shifter can change the way people look." Ari frowned. "That woman, the one that grabbed me first . . ."

"Kylie. The one who looks for you even now, with part of the evil army? One of His. Yes. She knows who you are. That's why she returned for you just now. And you have grown up since you've been gone, Arianna. You have changed. Many may not recognize you."

"My goodness." Ari put her hands to her head. Her mind was whirling. "The Shifter!" Rage welled up in Ari like a lava flow. Poor Lincoln! And she hadn't even had time to grieve! "My dog's been hurt." Tears flooded her eyes. "And Lady Kylie." The name sent a shiver of horror through her. "The Shifter's High Priestess."

"And your mother's friend. Before the Great Betrayal. Yes."

"My mother's friend! It can't be!"

"You will find the truth, Arianna. But it will take you a long time. Your memory will return slowly. It was lost in the terrible struggle. I do not know if you will ever regain it completely. And it may be at great cost to you and those you love."

The tears came back. Ari swallowed hard. Princesses didn't cry. Or did they? "There already has been a terrible cost. My dog is hurt, maybe dead! My family the same! I hate the Shifter! I hate him!"

"You must put aside your hate, Arianna. Hate will not save you or your people."

"Hate makes me strong," Ari said through clenched teeth.

"Hate blinds you. Hate is a tool of the Shifter." She laid her horn on Ari's shoulder. The crystal horn was a warm, living thing. With the touch of it, rage and terror ebbed out of Ari. Wondering, she raised her eyes to Atalanta. "You must listen to me, child. I haven't much time. Stand aside, please."

Ari slipped out of the way. As quiet as a whisper, Atalanta collected herself. She stood at attention, her neck arched, her hindquarters tucked, her back supple and slightly arched. And she sang, one long, lyrical note: "I call the Sunchaser."

"Chase." Ari stared at Atalanta. "Chase. *Chase is the Lord of the Unicorns!*"

Atalanta didn't reply. She stood as if carved in amethyst rock, her violet eyes on the open door to the stall.

Ari heard the distant sound of a horse jumping a fence: a short gallop, a moment of suspension, the moment of landing. Then she heard a familiar set of hoofbeats on the brick yard.

Chase appeared at the open door. He wasn't even breathing hard. His dark eyes searched and found Ari. Then he looked at the unicorn. Without a sound, he sank to his knees, great head bowed, forelegs knuckled against the straw.

"Sunchaser," Atalanta said. "It is hard to see you like this." She took a few steps toward him. The tip of her horn touched the scar on his forehead. Chase trembled. Sweat patched his withers. But he didn't lift his head.

"His horn is gone," Atalanta said sadly. "And his jewel is lost. Without them, he cannot hear me. Without them, he cannot speak."

Ari cleared her throat. Her voice was small and lost. "He can talk to me," she said.

Atalanta widened her violet eyes. "Indeed?"

"Yes. I hear him in my mind."

"Ah." The unicorn's tone was skeptical.

"It's true," Ari said. "Chase. Chase. Lift your head. Do you know who this is?"

A goddess, milady.

"He says you are a goddess," Ari informed her.

Atalanta looked thoughtful. "When did this happen?"

"On the other side of the Gap. At Glacier River Farm. At first I thought I was imagining it. And it only happened in moments when he was angry or upset."

"That is true of all horses, of all unicorns, whether they have personal magic or not," Atalanta said. "It is true in Balinor, and in all the worlds of humans and animals."

"But here," Ari insisted. "Here I can talk to him anytime." She added, politely, because Atalanta didn't seem to believe her, "It's true."

"If it is, then this is more of the magic I do not understand."

"There's magic *you* don't understand?"

"There is."

Ari swallowed. She had seen a little of the Shifter's magic, and it scared her. "Is it *bad* magic?"

"I don't know."

This was surprising and very unsettling. Atalanta smiled at Ari's expression. "There is a lot of magic about, Princess. Magic greater than my own. Even I must obey the laws of the One Who Rules humans and animals alike. Well, I must think about this. But it doesn't change the task you must accomplish."

"I think I know what it is. We have to find Chase's horn."

"Yes, Arianna. Without it, the people and animals of Balinor will lose all their ability to speak to one another. It is the unicorns who supply the link, you know. Between humankind and animals. Without you and the Sunchaser that link is broken."

"Okay," Ari said. "Where is it?"

"It was broken into several pieces. There is one here." Atalanta bent her head and nudged a nest of straw aside with her horn. A small stone glimmered in the white light shed by the unicorn's body.

Ari picked up the spiral stone with gentle fingers. "Why, I have two of these," she said. "I found them. . . . No, I believe now that someone — was it you? — wanted me to find them at Glacier River Farm." She fumbled in her skirt pocket. "Here." She withdrew the stones. "They were in two places: one in the south pasture, the other in Chase's grain." To her astonishment, two of the three pieces fit together.

"Samlett went through the Gap, at great risk to his own life, to leave these pieces for you. He hoped that once you touched them, felt them, that you would remember. There is magic in these pieces. He thought perhaps this magic would overcome the Shifter's work. Because it is the Shifter who made you forget. Do you know where the rest of the horn is?"

Ari's voice was hushed. "The Shifter has them."

"More or less." Atalanta's tone was dry. "The Sunchaser's horn was broken off in the battle on the day of the Great Betrayal. The day the King and Queen of Balinor were kidnapped, exiled. The day you yourself were sent to safety at Glacier River Farm, and the stallion with you."

Tears rolled down Ari's cheeks. Memories of her family and her life at the castle were tumbling back thick and fast now. But they were patchy, like morning fog on a river.

"Chase is the Lord of the Unicorns. And he is paired to you for life. But he cannot rule again — will not be himself again — until the horn has been restored to him."

"The Sunchaser is mine. My friend. My companion. The hereditary Lord of the Animals in Balinor." Ari pressed her hands to her temples, in an agony of thought. Would Chase become like Atalanta? Magical? Encased in celestial light? And if he did, would she lose the Chase she knew and loved right now?"

Ari blinked back tears. Atalanta's eyes were gentle. "The One Who Rules us all set the laws for us a long time ago, my dear. You are the Firstborn Princess. The Link to the Unicorn . . ."

"The Speaker for the animals here. And without me. Without Chase . . ."

"The power of speech is gone. The animals here will become like those at Glacier River. The world there is a world of humans only. When the great ice mountains moved through the world, so many millions of years ago, all humans and animals were linked in spirit. But a small part of that world was saved, split off, when the ice mountains plowed the land. The world on the other side of the Gap changed. Humans and animals lost the ability to speak to one another. But *not* in Balinor. Here, things are as they were at the beginning of time. And here, humans and animals are linked. By you. By the Sunchaser."

"Until the Shifter came."

"And if you do not do all you can to restore the Sunchaser's horn to him, this world will become like all the others. Where animals cannot speak. Where men are divided from nature. Where there is no magic at all."

Ari examined the three pieces of horn in her hand. She would set aside thoughts of losing Chase to magic. Her task now was to help him.

"You see this diamond at the base of my horn? This jewel contains a unicorn's personal magic. Without it, we are nothing. Without it, we are . . ." She paused. "Horses. Well enough for the world of humans. Not enough for Balinor."

"The ruby necklace?" Ari faltered. "Is Chase's magic in the ruby necklace?"

"Yes. The one you left behind."

"Oh, no! I had no idea! I have to go back and get it?"

"If you wish him to regain his power."

Ari couldn't look at the Dreamspeaker. And she couldn't ask the question that was tugging at her heart: Will he be the same? Will he be as remote from me as you are now, Dreamspeaker? She had no right to ask that question. Chase must regain his horn and his jewel. He had lost it. Without it, he would not be himself. And she couldn't deny him that. "I *must* go back and get it."

"If you can. Already the Shifter's army moves against us. The way to the Gap may be blocked."

"And the other pieces of the horn? Where are they?"

"The Sunchaser fought gallantly on the day of the Great Betrayal. His horn was splintered into four pieces. Mr. Samlett, who is a leader of the Resistance, picked up these three pieces and saved them to send to you. The other piece fell out of his hands."

"Fell where?"

"Near the Palace moat. The same Palace where the Shifter now rules through the Eye of Entia."

"I see now." Ari stood up as tall as she could. "What do I have to do, Atalanta? Tell me."

"Well!" said a sharp, all-too-familiar voice. "The first thing you can do is get that miserable Lori Carmichael down here. She's screaming her fool head off up in that room."

Ari whirled. Chase scrambled to his feet. A little woman with white hair and rosy cheeks stood foursquare in the doorway. A little of Atalanta's pure light reflected off her wire-rimmed glasses.

Ari sprang forward with a shout and gave her a huge hug. "Dr. Bohnes!" she cried. "Oh, Dr. Bohnes! Thank goodness you're here."

"Goodness has nothing to do with it," the vet said tartly. She turned a shy glance to Atalanta and bobbed an awkward curtsy. "Milady."

"Eliane," Atalanta said. "It's good to see you."

"It's wonderful to see you!" Ari burst out.

"Do you really think I'd leave you to your own devices? Who's going to rub your legs for you, so that they will get stronger and heal? And besides, I had to give you this." She dug into the pocket of her shabby shorts and held out her hand.

"Well, Eliane," Atalanta said. "I am pleased."

"Oh, Dr. Bohnes!" Ari's fingers shook as she picked it up. "The ruby necklace. You brought the ruby necklace!" It glowed brightly as she held it up. Chase brought his ears forward and looked at it attentively.

"You do not remember this?" Atalanta asked him.

Chase snorted. *Ari! She is speaking to me!*

"About the ruby, Chase. It is yours, after all. Do you recall how and where you lost it?"

He shook his head.

"I was afraid of this," Atalanta said. "It is going to make your quest that much more difficult, Sunchaser."

"What do we have to do?" Ari asked. "Just tell us, please, milady."

"It will be dangerous. But there's no help for it." Gradually, the glow around the Dreamspeaker had been getting more intense. It was becoming difficult to see her in the white light. Ari shaded her eyes with her hands. "I don't have much time, Arianna. Please listen. There is an old man on the far side of the woods — some two days' journey from here." The light grew brighter. All Ari could see now was the intense violet flare of the unicorn's eyes. Her silvery voice faded. "He is Minge, the Jewelwright. Take the necklace and the horn to him. He must fashion them together, make them as whole as he can . . . and then . . . the other piece at the Palace moat will join them. . . ."

She disappeared in a flare of radiance. The stall was dark. No one said anything for a moment. Then Dr. Bohnes clapped her hands together. "Come on, then. There's a great deal to do before morning."

7

"You're a what?" Lori demanded.

"Firstborn Princess, Link to the Unicorn, the Speaker for all the animals here." Dr. Bohnes's fingers were gentle as she probed Linc's still body. He was breathing, but just barely. Ari watched, her hands clenched so hard the nails dug into her palms. Ari and the vet had sneaked quietly into the Inn after putting Chase back in his paddock. They'd taken Linc upstairs to Lori's bedroom. There, as Dr. Bohnes had said, Lori was having a major temper tantrum.

When the noise of the attack on Ari broke out, Lori had dragged the big chest across the room to barricade her door, then crawled under the bed to hide. At first, she'd been so glad to see Ari and Dr. Bohnes that for a minute, she'd behaved like a nice, normal person. Then Dr. Bohnes had told her briefly what the riot had been all about.

"I don't believe it! A Princess? Get real!" But her eyes wouldn't meet Ari's. And she backed away from her. "And this . . . this unicorn with the magic that told you all this stuff. Where is she now?"

"Gone back to the Celestial Valley," Dr. Bohnes said. "Her kind aren't allowed to stay here long. Well." She got up and dusted her knees. "That was a crack on the head, to be sure. He's alive, but just barely. It's going to take awhile for that head to heal."

"Can you do something?" Ari asked softly. Lovingly, she stroked the cream and bronze fur. Linc's eyes were closed, his breathing deep and slow.

"Time is all he needs. You know what that's like. It took awhile for those legs of yours to get as good as they are now. And I wouldn't call them one hundred percent."

Ari dropped her head in her hands. She was so tired. And there was so much to do! "This is impossible, Dr. Bohnes."

"Not impossible. And it's a lot to ask of anyone. But we have to do it. We have to. For if the Shifter wins . . ." For a moment, the sparkle drained out of the old vet's face. Ari had never thought of Dr. Bohnes as old. She was always filled with life and energy, striding around, snapping out orders, her tough old hands amazingly gentle when they massaged Ari's hurt legs. But now — the wrinkles in her face were deep. The skin beneath her bright blue

72

eyes sagged. "Do you know me, child? I know you don't remember everything yet. You won't. Not until the Sunchaser gets his horn back and the two of you return to the way you were meant to be. Bonded for life. But do you remember me?"

"Why, yes," Ari said slowly. "I think I do. You were my nurse."

"And Chase's caretaker."

"That's right. And . . ." Ari smiled a little. "My father called you 'a little bit of a wizard.'"

"More than a little. Yes, Arianna, I am a wizard. Not enough, I'm afraid, to protect you entirely when we start our journey to the forest's edge tomorrow. And my power's getting less as that devil Shifter's power grows here." She sat heavily on the bed and rubbed her back. "Old bones," she sighed.

Ari sat down next to her and rubbed Dr. Bohnes's back and shoulders, just as the vet had rubbed Ari's own legs. "Is that better?"

"No, it's not better," she said sharply. "Nothing's going to be better until your mother and father are back on the throne, and you and Chase are bonded again. Nothing's going to be better until the Shifter is driven back to the Caves beneath the Six Seas." A reluctant grin brought some of the sparkle back. "But your hands are young and strong. And that does feel good on my old bones. And we aren't down yet! Not by a long shot."

At Dr. Bohnes's insistence, they settled down to sleep, even though morning was close. The vet and Lori shared the bed. Ari rolled up the borrowed cloak and lay near the collie. She drifted off to sleep, troubled by dreams of a searching Eye. She woke with a start, staring straight into a pair of brown eyes.

"Linc!" She got on her knees and softly stroked the collie's ears. "How are you feeling, boy?"

My head hurts.

"I'm sure it does. Don't try to get up. I'm going to get you a little more water and a bit of breakfast. You have to eat, you know." She got to her feet and rubbed the sleep out of her eyes. Pale light came through the window. She looked out. Rain today, if she was any judge. Dr. Bohnes snapped awake and rolled out of bed, grumbling. She grabbed her backpack and stamped out the door to the washroom.

Ari pulled on her boots and brushed her hair. None of them had had the strength to get out of their clothes the night before, and she felt grubby. "Lori?" she asked quietly. "You awake?"

"Uh! Leave me alone."

"I'm going to ask Mr. Samlett for some food for Linc. Will you watch him? Hold his head if he gets sick. Dr. Bohnes said that happens with a concussion."

"You want me to hold the dog's head if he barfs? Aagh!" She sat up. She was a mess. Tears from the night before had smeared on her cheeks. The scowl on her face didn't improve her looks at all.

74

"I won't be long. Then you can wash up."

"Okay, okay." She brought her knees up to her chin and wrapped her arms around her legs. She was frowning, but at least she was frowning at Linc.

Ari slipped downstairs and went into the pantry. It was early. Mr. Samlett was already in the kitchen unloading a basket of eggs in a wooden bowl on the big table in the middle of the kitchen. He dropped one on the floor as Ari came into the room.

"Oops!" Ari said. "Hang on, Mr. Samlett. I'll clean that up."

"Milady! Oh! Milady!" He waved his hands in the air. Two more eggs rolled off the table and smashed on the flagstones. It was getting to be quite a mess. What was this milady stuff from Mr. Samlett? Ari glanced over her shoulder. Had Lori come down? She was going to get a good talking to if she'd left Linc alone. Nope. Lori wasn't there. She turned back to see Mr. Samlett on his knees in front of her. "Forgive me," he sobbed. "Oh, forgive me! And I said you were such a good stable hand! The best, I said, and you the Princess." Big tears ran down his red cheeks.

Ari bit back a laugh. "Now, Mr. Samlett. Who told you?"

"Eliane Bohnes!" he sobbed. "Just now. She's out in the yard getting a cart ready for you. I say a cart ready for you. A cart! That's all you ask of me. A cart! And I called you the —"

"The best stable hand you'd ever had. Please

get off your knees, Mr. Samlett. It feels really weird to have you down there." She extended a hand to help him up. He got to his feet with a groan. "Now, I understand I have you to thank for many things, Mr. Samlett. You helped me through the Gap. You saved as much of the Sunchaser's horn as you could. And this Inn is the heart of those loyal to my father and mother and me. I have one more thing to thank you for. Do you know what it is?"

He shook his head woefully.

"For giving me a job when I needed one!"

His eyes went wide. Then he began to chuckle. The chuckle turned into a laugh. He was still laughing when Dr. Bohnes stumped into the room.

"Put a cork in it, Samlett," Dr. Bohnes said. "We're going to need provisions for a three-day journey in addition to that cart."

"Three days? You and Her Highness are leaving?! You can't!"

"Hush!" the old vet commanded. "You keep Arianna's return to yourself, if you please. It's far too dangerous here as it is. You must not tell a living soul, Samlett. Do you understand? All our lives are at stake."

Samlett bowed to Ari. He was completely serious now. "I do, Eliane."

"All right, then. I'm going to take you upstairs, Samlett. You'll have to take care of Linc the dog while we're gone. I want to show you what to do."

Mr. Samlett's lower lip stuck out like a baby's. "But the dog doesn't talk!"

"So? It's one of nature's creatures. And deserving of your compassion. Eh, Samlett?"

"He talks to me, Mr. Samlett," Ari said quietly. "He's from beyond the Gap. The place where you and the others took me to save me from the Shifter. And even if he couldn't talk, I would not want to be Princess of a Kingdom where one being was considered more worthy than another."

"Well put," Dr. Bohnes said. "Now, if you're finished being Royal, Ari, get your rear in gear. The sooner we find that Jewelwright, the better!"

The next half hour passed in a flurry of activity. Mr. Samlett swore to call the Guild of Balinor Dog Physicians if Linc became the slightest bit worse. Ari prepared food for the journey and packed a small kit of brushes and hoof picks for Chase. Dr. Bohnes had not only commandeered Samlett's best cart, but cajoled the spotted unicorn Toby into pulling it.

Lori dawdled around the fringes and sulked. "How long are you going to be gone?" she asked for the umpteenth time.

Ari was just about finished in the kitchen. She added a second bag of dried fruit to the pack she was loading. Weight shouldn't be too much of a problem if they were driving, rather than hiking. And it wouldn't do to run out of food. Dr. Bohnes had suggested they travel the out-of-the-way roads, because no one knew where the Shifter's forces were. And it was easier to hide evil in large towns than small ones.

"Ari?" Lori demanded. "Or don't you answer to anything but 'Your Highness' these days?" She swept a mock curtsy.

"Sorry, Lori. I was counting dried apples. Dr. Bohnes isn't exactly sure where we have to go. But she thinks it's near here. I'll show you." She pulled out of the backpack the small map of Balinor that Mr. Samlett had given them.

"We travel through the forest —"

"The same one we came through when we landed in this forsaken place? Where those so-called bears were?"

"There isn't any other way to get south," Ari said. "From there, we go through what Mr. Samlett called 'a bit of a swamp' and what Dr. Bohnes called a 'mucky bog.' I don't know anything about it, to tell you the truth. If I ever did, I don't remember. Anyhow, we come out into the small village of Luckon. It's quite near the Palace, I understand. So if we can get Chase's jewel and horn repaired . . ." She trailed off. After the jewel and the part of the horn in her possession were merged, she and Chase would have to go to the Palace to find the last part of the horn.

She shook the thought away.

"Anyway," she finished briskly. "That's it."

"So I suppose I'll come along," Lori said sulkily.

Ari's mouth dropped open. "You? Are you sure you want to?"

"Why not? Do you expect me to stay here? Without money? That Samlett character said he'd give me a room, all right. As long as I mucked out stalls and scrubbed the kitchen floor. Forget that."

"But, Lori. It might be dangerous."

"Old Bohnes is a wizard, isn't she? And who's going to mess with a Princess? That is, if you are a Princess, which I don't believe for one second flat. Besides . . ." She muttered something Ari couldn't catch.

"Sorry. I didn't hear you."

"I said I'm scared to stay here by myself. I saw those creeps go after you last night. If those jerks come looking for a thirteen-year-old girl and find one, they aren't going to believe me when I tell them it isn't me."

"Mr. Samlett knows."

"Phooey. And frankly, Ari, who looks more like a Princess? You or me? I don't want to risk staying here alone, thank you very much."

Ari shrugged. "Suit yourself. I guess I'd better add a little more food."

The sun was over the eastern hills by the time they were ready to go. Toby backed himself into the shafts of the little cart Mr. Samlett had given them. It was bright blue, with two wheels and a sign on the side that read: THE UNICORN INN FINE EATS! Dr. Bohnes hopped onto the double seat and took the reins.

Lori climbed in and sat beside her. Mr. Samlett loaded the last of the packs into the back of the cart. Ari, who had saddled and bridled Chase with the tack that had come from Glacier River Farm, swung into the saddle with difficulty. Her legs were more than usually cramped this morning. She saw Dr. Bohnes eyeing her, but the old vet didn't say a word.

"Milady!" Mr. Samlett tugged shyly on her stirrup. Ari looked down at him. "Take this," he whispered. "Just in case." He drew a thin leather scabbard out of his sleeve and slipped it into the top of her boot. "It was your father's."

She caught the glitter of a gold-encrusted hilt. A powerful memory swept her: a tall man, broad-shouldered, his blond head thrown back in laughter. His well-shaped hands pared an apple. He cut off a slice and offered it to her on the blade of his knife.

This knife. Her father's.

She stared down at the scabbard, which was almost completely hidden by the top of her boot. She touched the ruby jewel, concealed beneath her skirt. She set her jaw. She tapped her heels into Chase's side and rode to the head of the cart. "Move on out, Toby. We're ready."

8

The blue cart and its passengers didn't get a lot of attention as they rode through the village on their way to the forest. Ari and her hornless unicorn did, however.

Dr. Bohnes drew to a halt in front of a thatched three-sided shed. Bunches of dried herbs hung from the shelves. Bottles with mysterious contents stood in disarray on the counter facing the dirt street. A thin woman with curly brown hair and serious gray eyes was sitting on a stool as the procession stopped. She got up and dropped a polite, perfunctory curtsy. The sort of curtsy, Ari realized, that was part of the general manners of these villagers. She was on horseback — or rather, unicorn-back — so she nodded in return.

"I have nothing to help you, miss," she said. "And never have I seen such a thing. A hornless unicorn! What terrible times we live in."

81

"We didn't stop for that," Dr. Bohnes said gruffly. "How are you, Leia?"

The woman bent forward. Her eyes widened. Dr. Bohnes raised a cautionary finger to her lips. "Eliane! Is it you?" she whispered.

Dr. Bohnes nodded, and said loudly, "Mistress Leia, I've heard you have fine teas for sale. I would like some peppermint, if you please."

"Why — ah — certainly, Eli . . . Mo . . . I mean, madam. Will you come to the back with me? You can make your own selection there."

"Ari?" Dr. Bohnes motioned her off Chase with a commanding forefinger. Ari dismounted and followed the two women into the depths of the shed.

Once out of the sight of passersby, Dr. Bohnes gave Mistress Leia a quick hug. "It's good to see you well."

"And you, Eliane! I'm glad to see that you are safe. I've heard such terrible rumors!"

"That's why I've stopped to see you. You know more about what's going on in Balinor than any ten Samletts. I need to know what lies in the way of our getting to see old Minge."

"The Jewelwright?" Leia's eyebrows drew together in a frown. "Why would you want to see him?" She went on, with a rush, "Is it true, Eliane? That the Princess is lost, perhaps dead? That the Sunchaser has lost his jewel?" She gasped. Her hands went to her mouth. Her gray eyes met Ari's blue ones. "Your

82

Highness!" she exclaimed. She sank to the floor in a profound bow.

"Oh, my," Ari said uncomfortably. It was hard getting used to this. She hoped every single person they met wasn't going to drop to the dirt like a lopped-off cabbage every time her identity was revealed. On second thought, she'd be glad if the Shifter and his gruesome pals did that instead of trying to cut off her own head like a cabbage.

"Please get up, ma'am," Ari said.

Leia raised her head. There were tears in her eyes. "We thought we would never see you again!" she said softly. "Your mother, the Queen? Your father?"

"We don't know anything at the moment, Leia," Dr. Bohnes said briskly. "Now, get up and give us the news, there's a good woman. Where is the Demon herd? And what about Sistern?"

Sistern. Another memory rocked Ari. Tentacles. A huge beak. One single yellow-green eye. A scaly, slimy thing that could travel in water as fast as it could on land. She drew a shaky breath.

"No one's heard a thing about the Demon unicorns, not since they passed through the King's forest yesterday."

"And they were headed north," Dr. Bohnes murmured. "We are headed south."

"Sistern now dwells in the moat outside the Palace." Leia shuddered. "They say he was maimed in the battle on the day of the Great Betrayal. That he can no longer walk on land. That is why . . ." She bit her lip. Her face was pale.

"Why what?" Dr. Bohnes demanded.

"That is why the Shadow King flies at night."

"What's this? The Shifter has bred a new monster? With wings?"

"They say it's the Eye of Entia. In a new and more horrible form. The Eye can see far now, above the land. Perhaps to the gates of the Celestial Valley itself."

"Have you seen this winged Shadow?"

"Once. I didn't see it as much as I felt it passing. Like a cold, cold wind, Mother Eliane. And I could not move for fear."

"Humph." Dr. Bohnes tugged at her lower lip. "That's all the news?"

"All except this." She turned to Ari and curtsied a third time. "We are so glad for your return, Your Highness. The hearts of the people are with you."

"We'll need more than their hearts before this is over," Dr. Bohnes said bitingly. "Keep the news about Arianna to yourself for the moment, Leia. But when the time comes . . ."

"When the time comes . . ." Leia echoed. She raised her fist in the air. "We will fight!"

9

"We will fight," Ari murmured to herself. They were deep in the forest. The air was still. Dark was coming on, and Dr. Bohnes was on the lookout for shelter from the moonless night. They had taken the wrong turn a few hours back.

"You said we wouldn't have to spend the night here," Lori complained. She drew her cloak around her and shivered. "I'm freezing."

"The worst possible night to be out with the Shifter's forces looking for you," Dr. Bohnes said to Ari. She jiggled the reins over Toby's back. "Step out, Toby. That shepherd's hut can't be too far from here."

"Your directions were awful," the unicorn threw over his back. "Past the cove of pine trees, you said. Then north by northeast, you said."

"I was right," Dr. Bohnes said flatly. "It's you who can't tell north from south, Toby."

The unicorn stopped in his tracks. "Hey!" His voice had the patient reasonableness parents use with idiot children. "You face north, right? If you face north, south is in back of you. East is to the left of you."

"East is to the right of you," Dr. Bohnes said. "I told you before."

"Left! Left! Left!" Toby stamped his right fore-foot each time he hollered. Ari burst into laughter. "And what's so funny?" Toby asked icily.

"You are," Lori said. "I've never seen such a boneheaded unicorn in my life. For one thing, you can't even tell your left foot from your right foot, which means nobody can understand how we got so lost in the first place, because when you were wrong you were right."

"Right here," a scratchy voice said.

Everyone jumped.

"Where did that come from?" Lori demanded.

"From the bush. Over there. To your *left*," Toby said sourly.

Ari looked to her right. The bushes twitched.

It's a human, Chase said. *And beyond him, I think I sense the shepherd's hut.*

"How can you sense a shepherd's hut?" Ari asked.

The wind blows around its shape. And there are movements in the forest. Vibrations on the floor.

The vibrations change when there is a structure there. I feel those movements through my hooves.

"Right here," the voice said again. The brush parted. A man with wild hair and a very dirty face peered at them dubiously. "You who I bin expectin'?"

"Whom have you been expecting?" Dr. Bohnes sounded grim.

"Travelers. In need of a place to sleep. They say you'll pay."

"Who says?" Lori asked sharply. "And if you don't take Visa, forget it. I don't have any money, and they don't, either."

"Them." The man jerked his chin up. Ari craned her head back and looked into the trees. A flock of crows hopped silently overhead. One of them blinked his beady eye at her and said, "Toll! Pay the toll! Pay the toll!"

"We have a few pennies," Dr. Bohnes said. "Is the place clean?"

"Yes'm."

"And do you have water?"

"Yes'm."

"Then we accept your offer of hospitality."

"Huh?"

"We'll pay," Lori clarified. Then, not so quietly that he couldn't hear it, "Moron!"

The grimy man said his name was Tomlett. This appeared to reassure Dr. Bohnes, who questioned him at length about his family as he led the way through the forest to the shepherd's hut.

"He's a member of one of the Forest Clans," she said as they settled inside the hut. The old vet had made a brief inspection of the hut, informed Tomlett in no uncertain terms that it wasn't clean enough, and sent him off to draw water. "A distant relative of Samlett's, in fact."

"That's all right, then," Ari said.

"Maybe," Dr. Bohnes said, "and maybe not. Most of the Forest Clans are independent. They couldn't give a hoot about who hangs around the Palace." She rubbed her hands together. "Lori. Get the dried apples and the corn pancakes from the packs and serve the food."

"Me!" Lori said indignantly.

"You. Ari will see to the unicorns. I'm going to take a nap." She sat down and leaned against the wall with a groan. "These old bones," she said. "These old bones." She dropped asleep instantly.

Ari went outside to make sure that Toby and Chase had enough forage for the night. Lori came out of the hut grumbling, and unloaded the packs from the cart. Toby was still hitched. Chase grazed restlessly next to him. Ari went over and began to unbuckle the lines from the shafts of the cart. Toby stamped his foot and said, "Stop."

"Do you have a stone in your hoof?" Ari asked. "Let me get the hoof pick."

"No stone. There's something going on I don't like."

Without thinking, Ari's hand went to the knife in her boot. "What is it?" she whispered softly.

"Look up."

Ari gazed upward.

"Don't be so obvious about it, Princess!" Toby said.

Ari rubbed her nose casually. She stretched her neck this way and that. She rolled her shoulders, put her arms over her head, and yawned.

All the while she battled fear. "The crows," she whispered to Toby. "There are thousands of them in the trees. And Toby, their eyes . . ." She shuddered.

"Demon eyes," Toby agreed quietly. "They've found us. Or Tomlett's betrayed us. Get those two out of the hut and into the cart."

Ari? Chase stood at full alert, gazing into the trees. *There is danger here.*

"Would you tell him not to hang out a *sign!*" Toby grumbled. "Tell him to keep on grazing, like nothing's happening. If those birds attack . . ."

"What do they want?" Ari whispered back. She caught the eye of a large crow. It glittered like a banked coal. His pinfeathers stuck up all over his back. He chattered at her, "Pay the toll! Pay the toll! PAY THE JEWEL!"

Ari stopped herself just in time. She almost grabbed the jewel around her neck. And if they saw where it was hidden, the birds would attack for certain.

"Food's ready," Lori announced. She stood at the door to the hut.

"Get Dr. Bohnes," Ari said as normally as she could.

"She's asleep."

"There's something wrong with Toby's hoof."

The black-and-white unicorn nodded vigorously. The harness jingled wildly as he shook his head. "I want a doctor NOW!" he said.

"Oh, all right!" Lori flounced into the hut and a few moments later, Dr. Bohnes stumbled out. She yawned, scratched her head, and stamped over to Toby. "Which foot is it? Right or left. What the heck am I asking you for, you don't know the dif —"

Ari grabbed her hand and squeezed it. The vet's bright blue eyes narrowed. Ari jerked her chin upward, ever so slightly. Dr. Bohnes nodded. "Lori," she said curtly, "get the hoof pick and bring it to me. Right now."

"I'm eating!"

"And this unicorn's lame. Move it."

"Aaagh!" Lori slammed back into the hut.

"Bring the whole pack, Lori," Ari suggested in what she hoped was a casual tone. Her palms were sweating. She wiped them down the sides of her breeches. Chase, who had been grazing nearer and nearer in ever-smaller circles, nudged her in the back with his muzzle.

We must ride, milady. We don't have much time.

"Oh, Lor-ri!" Ari looked up in pretended exasperation. She probed the trees as she chattered. Hundreds of crows gathered in the trees above. Perhaps thousands. What unnerved her most was the silence in which the birds gathered. All except one. The bird with the demon eyes, who chattered, "Pay the toll! Pay the toll! PAY THE JEWEL!"

"Here!" Lori thumped the backpack on the ground.

"Move!" Ari shouted. In one fluid motion, she drew her father's knife from her boot and leaped onto Chase's back. Dr. Bohnes clambered into the wagon and jerked Lori after her by her long blond hair. As soon as he felt their weight in the cart, Toby took off at a dead run.

And the crows attacked. Screaming, cawing, their wings were like a tidal wave. They flew down from the trees straight at Ari and Chase. The great stallion reared, and Ari realized with a pang that he was trying to spear the birds with his horn. But he had no horn! She stabbed upward with her father's knife, slashing the air.

A memory flooded her. She was in a high, white room. Her brother was there. He held a stick in his hands. "Thrust home!" he cried.

"Thrust home!" Ari yelled. She sliced at a huge bird flying straight toward Chase's eyes. Feathers fluttered into her hair. "We must run, Chase!"

I. Do. Not. Run. From. Battle!

"You have no horn!" Ari shrieked. She slammed her heels into his sides. Shocked, Chase took a great leap forward. The crows rose in a whirlwind after them, cawing. Ari slammed her heels into him again. "Run!"

They raced off after the cart. Chase thundered through the woods, dodging trees, leaping over fallen logs, splashing through pools of water. The forest grew denser. Thicker. The crows fell behind. Ari could hear their frustrated shrieks. But the trees were too thick for the birds to penetrate without getting caught in the branches. Chase slowed to a walk. His great sides heaved in and out. His withers were covered with sweat. Ari bent forward and patted his neck. He stopped and quivered.

Do you hear that?

"What?" She held her breath. She heard shouts, ahead of them through the trees. "It's Toby and the others! They're in trouble!"

They raced through the trees to try to save the others.

10

Toby had run straight into the swamp. He was just a few feet from shore when he realized they were sinking. The mud was thick and sucked at his hooves with a slow, inexorable force. He thrashed slowly, and with purpose. Lori clung to the sides of the cart and screamed.

Ari pulled Chase up just in time. His left forefoot slipped into the muck. He pulled it free with a surge of his powerful muscles. Ari slipped off her stallion and stood in despair.

"Do something!" Lori screamed. "We're sinking!"

"I can see that," Ari said. Dr. Bohnes, her hands steady on the reins, looked at her and smiled. "Do you think you can throw the lines to me? I can tie them to Chase's saddle and he can pull you backward."

"Too heavy, even for him," Dr. Bohnes said. The cart slipped further into the ooze. "Pull Lori out first."

"But . . ."

"No buts. The way she's wriggling around, she's making us sink faster."

"Lori," Ari called. "LORI!"

"What!"

"I'm going to throw Chase's reins to you!"

"I'm going to die!"

Ari gave up trying to talk to her. She was glad now, that she never had to use a bit with Chase. He was wearing a nose band, a head stall, and nothing more. She just hoped the leather would hold. She searched the ground beneath her feet for a heavy rock. She found it. She tied the end of the reins around it, and tossed it into the cart. It hit Dr. Bohnes on the back. The old vet slumped forward. Ari stood frozen in fear. Dr. Bohnes shook her head and then reached around and handed the reins to Lori.

The cart sank another twelve inches into the muck. Toby was still struggling gallantly. His muzzle was just above the slime.

Lori held onto the reins, too scared now to scream.

"Okay, Chase," Ari said.

The great stallion pulled back. Lori flew out of the cart and landed half in and half out of the mud. Ari pulled her to her feet, took the reins, and threw them out again to Dr. Bohnes.

The vet crawled forward and tied the reins around the shafts of the cart.

"Dr. Bohnes! Bohnesy!" Ari clenched her fists to keep from screaming.

"We can't leave him here," Dr. Bohnes said. "And there's no one to tie the reins to him once I'm out."

"You. Go. Ahead," Toby said. His voice was thick with mud.

"Okay, boy," Ari said. "Pull!"

Chase backed up. He tugged. The cart moved up, then settled back into the swamp.

"For me, Chase. For me!"

Chase pulled again. The muscles swelled on his haunches and sweat broke out on his neck. His eyes bulged with effort. The cart rose and sank, then rose and sank again. Slowly, miraculously, it started to come out of the swamp. Chase pulled steadily. Ari was afraid to look at Toby, but she couldn't look away. The black-and-white unicorn was almost completely under the mud. All she could see was his horn, sticking bravely up, like a flag.

"Hurry, Chase! He can't survive under there very long!"

Blood ran out of Chase's nose. The edge of the cart reached firm ground. Dr. Bohnes quickly climbed out to safety.

Ari grabbed the edge of the cart with both hands and cried, "Pull, both of you. Pull!"

They all put their backs into it. Finally, the cart rolled free. Ari leaped forward, but she was too late. The reins slipped off the shafts.

Toby was gone, except for the tip of his horn.

Ari wound the reins around her waist, and plunged into the swamp. She sank to her chest almost immediately. Dr. Bohnes's hands were firmly around her shoulders. Lori grabbed her right arm. With her left, she searched under the mud. After a few terrible moments, she found a leather strap, and a warm hide underneath. "I've got him!" she gasped. She tied the reins around the belly band of the harness.

"Pull!" Dr. Bohnes shouted. "Pull for your lives!"

With a tremendous groan of pain, Chase dragged Toby out of the swamp.

The spotted unicorn lay dreadfully still. Dr. Bohnes took the edge of her shirt and quickly wiped the mud from his nose and mouth. His eyes were closed. "But he's still breathing," Lori said timidly. "Look!"

It was true. His flanks heaved in and out with the harshest of breaths. Dr. Bohnes crouched over him for a long anxious moment. Then his eyes flickered open. He gave a great cough. Swamp mud poured out of his mouth and all over Lori's feet. The blond girl crouched down and smoothed the fore-lock away from Toby's eyes.

"You — told — me — to — take — a — left!" He coughed.

Then he gave a sigh and fell peacefully asleep.

They were delayed two days while Toby re-covered. Ari wanted to ride Chase to the nearest village for help, but Dr. Bohnes refused with a curt shake of her head. "We must all stick together now," she said.

"We don't have enough food for three days," Ari said.

"Skimpy rations aren't going to bother *me*. They'll have to do."

Lori opened her mouth to whine, looked at poor Toby lying asleep on the grass, and shut it.

And from there on in, she stopped complain-ing. Ari was amazed. She helped clean the cart, helped wash out their clothes, and even helped Ari wash her hair.

Finally, Toby coughed up the last of the swamp mud, and they proceeded around the swamp to the village of Luckon, where the Jewelwright Minge lived.

"Except he don't live here no more," the Innkeeper of Luckon said. The Inn was situated on the outskirts of the village. Lori greeted the prospect of a hot bath with a squeal of relief. As Dr. Bohnes disbursed the necessary funds to the Innkeeper, Lori ran upstairs to take a bath. Toby and Chase relaxed in the outside paddock, eating good green hay for the first time in almost a week.

"Sure he does," the serving girl grunted. "He lives somewhere around here. He comes in here all the time."

"Every day?" Ari asked.

"Sure. Most weeks. Sometimes every other day." The serving girl had bright red hair and a lot of freckles. She also talked a lot. She talked incessantly for the next three days, while Dr. Bohnes, Chase, Ari, and Lori waited for the Jewelwright. Toby, much quieter since his near-death experience, slept a great deal.

On the morning of the fourth day, Dr. Bohnes told Ari their funds were running out. "And I don't like being in one place for too long," she added. "Word travels fast, even in country villages like these. And you know that the Palace isn't all that far away."

"Is it?" Ari asked vaguely. Not much of her memory had returned. "Have I ever been in Luckon?"

"Once. Long time ago. Just before the Ceremony of the Bonding." Her wise eyes wrinkled in thought. "You don't remember that?"

"With Chase, you mean. No, I don't remember that. And Dr. Bohnes, I'm worried. His . . . his speech seems to be going. I mean, I can't really talk with him anymore."

Dr. Bohnes nodded. "Doesn't surprise me."

"Isn't there anything we can do?" Ari got up and moved restlessly around the Inn. This place was not nearly as comfortable as the Unicorn Inn in Balinor. The wood floors were never clear of straw and mud. And the food was awful.

"Nothing," Dr. Bohnes said. "We can do nothing without the jewel and mended horn."

11

Numinor, the Golden One, went down the hill at an impatient walk, his hooves striking sparks from the granite gravel on his way. The unicorns of the Celestial herd raised their heads at his approach, then melted silently into the trees when they saw how he looked.

"Atalanta!" he called out. "Atalanta!" He jumped the huge bore of a fallen tree with an angry flick of his tail.

"I am here, milord." The Dreamspeaker moved as she always did, quietly, gracefully, like a flower on a stream, but she seemed tired, and her eyes were cloudy.

Numinor snorted, then reared. He came to earth with a thump. "And I am here, and so are all the others! *But where is the Jewelwright?*"

"I have looked. I have watched. I cannot see him."

Numinor's great golden head sank against his chest. For a moment, he said nothing. "Then what more can we do? Is it time for us to march? Has the Shifter taken the Jewelwright? Must we follow the Path from the Moon to Balinor, an army which that world has never seen before?"

"Others have gone that way, milord. They have left the Valley on the Path from the Moon, and have gone below." She said no more, but waited.

"The Demon herd, you mean."

"Yes. Pride, milord. A fatal thing, especially in Kings."

Numinor raised his head to the setting sun. The Shifter's Moon was done for another month, and now the Unicorn Moon, the Silver Traveler herself, shone brightly even as the sun went down. "They left, the dark ones of the rainbow. And were not allowed to return." He dropped his head and looked intently at the Dreamspeaker. "How shall we know? How shall we know, Atalanta, when it is time to march? What if I make the mistake that *he* —"

"Hush," Atalanta said. "We will not speak of it now."

Numinor raised his left foreleg to strike the ground, then visibly restrained himself. "Where is that Jewelwright?" he trumpeted. "I command that you appear!"

Atalanta looked at him, a grave expression in

her eyes. He could command all he liked, the Golden One. But the Jewelwright listened to his own music and played his own tune.

Like Arianna and Chase, the unicorns must wait.

12

The fourth day at the Inn in Luckon dragged on. Finally, just as the sun was setting, a little old man plodded up to the Inn on an incredibly ancient unicorn.

It was a mare. But an old, old mare. Older than her master, it seemed. Both of them had hair sticking out of their ears, grizzly beards, and sway-backs. The old man gave her neck a pat, then walked into the Inn.

"Hey!" the red-haired serving girl said. "There he is. Minge. Where you been?"

"Out," the old man said. He settled himself on a bench under the window.

"You want coffee?"

"What d'ya think I want. River water?"

This sent both of them into giggles.

"Say," the serving girl said. "There's some folks been looking for you."

"That right?"

"Um. Over there." She jerked her thumb toward Lori and Ari, who were staring openmouthed at him. This was Minge, the Jewelwright?

Minge ambled over. He wore baggy pants, a floppy hat, and a patched gray shirt. "Hey," he said.

"Hey, yourself," Lori replied. She looked at Ari. Ari looked at her. They both burst into giggles.

"You folks have a job for me?"

Ari's giggles died away. "Yes," she said soberly. "I do." She pulled the ruby necklace from around her neck, drew it over her head, and held it in her palm.

Minge bent over her hand. His breath tickled her palm. He smelled like tobacco, sweat, and tired food. "Uh-huh," he said. "That's a unicorn's jewel, that is." He backed up and looked at her. His eyes were gray and very, very wise. They were amazingly youthful in his ancient face. "You have something else for me, then."

"Yes." Ari pulled the three pieces of Chase's horn out of her pocket. "Do you . . . can you . . . it's so important, Mr. Minge."

"Yuh. Hang on, just a second." He took both the jewel and the pieces of horn from Ari. He tottered back to his bench, where the red-haired serving girl stood with a tankard of coffee. Ari started forward, in protest. Minge drained the tankard, wiped his mouth firmly with the back of his hand, then tottered back to where the girls were sitting.

He sat down close to Ari. He held his hands out, the jewel in the left hand, the horn in the right. Slowly, he brought his hands together. A puff of crimson smoke escaped from his clasped palms. He opened his hands.

The jewel held the half horn like a candlestick holds a candle.

"He out back?"

Ari knew who Minge meant. "Yes. In the paddock."

She and Lori followed the old man out the door and around to the small fenced area that had been Chase's home for the past few days. The great stallion's coat was dull, his eyes remote. When Ari tried to talk to him now, he listened with a puzzled air, as if hearing the murmur of wind or water. If she had any doubts about restoring his horn to him, they were long past. She couldn't stand to see him this way.

Chase raised his head as they approached.

"Well, now," Minge said. "Well, now." He eased himself through the paddock gate and walked up to Chase. He passed his left hand over the stallion's face, then put his right hand on the white scar.

He stepped back.

Chase shook his head, bewildered. He opened his eyes. He looked full at Ari, his eyes dark and full of feeling. And he spoke to her, his voice strong and resonant with feeling. "Milady," he said, "I have returned to you."

13

Clouds obscured the moon outside the Sunchaser's paddock. Ari walked as silently as she could. Dr. Bohnes had made her take off her riding boots — too noisy and the noise might attract the enemy! — and replace them with soft sandals. Nobody had been able to find any clean socks, so Ari's toes were bare. Her feet were cold. She wore her breeches, a clean white blouse, and the leather vest.

She tried not to jump at the normal nighttime sounds: the scrabble of small creatures in the brush, the sweep of an owl's wings, the shifting of branches in the evening breeze.

"Chase?" Ari whispered.

"I'm here, milady." His great shape moved toward her, a darker shadow in the night. The moonlight glimmered softly off the horn on his forehead. She could see the jagged edge where the final piece would go.

If they found it.

If they returned alive.

Chase bent and breathed into her hair. Ari slipped her arms around his neck. "We go for the rest of your horn tonight," she said into his ear. "And it's a terribly dangerous thing to do."

"I am with you, milady. As always."

"I brought sacking with me, Chase. I must tie the bags around your feet, to muffle the sound of your hooves." She stood with her back to his head. She ran her hand down his foreleg and pinched lightly behind the coronet band, just as she did when she cleaned his foot with the hoof pick. He lifted his forefoot immediately and rested it on her bended knee. She worked rapidly, not wanting him to know how painful this was to her scarred muscles. She slipped the burlap bag over his hoof, wound baling twine several times around his ankle, then tied it off in a knot. She slipped a finger between the twine and his skin, to make sure it wasn't too tight. Unicorns, like horses, were very vulnerable to swollen legs if their hooves were wrapped too tight. She muffled all four hooves in turn, then straightened up with a sigh. Dr. Bohnes had wanted to massage her legs; she had missed her regular sessions. There just wasn't time.

He knelt before her, the iron-hard legs folding gracefully under his belly. She slipped onto his back and tapped her heels lightly into his sides. He rose like a ship pitching on the waves, bringing his haunches well underneath him, and rising to stand tall. Ari settled herself onto his back. Yes, there was the slight depression behind his withers that just fit her long legs. She straightened her back and brought her seat well under her. She flexed her knees and Chase walked out.

"Shall we jump the fence?"

"Too noisy," Ari said quietly. "Are you ready?"

"I am."

They moved out quietly. The sound of his muffled hooves was very faint on the dirt path. Dr. Bohnes had explained the directions to the Palace over and over again. "You must be silent," she had said. "The Shifter's beings are all around your old home."

Home! Ari thought. Am I really headed home? She wouldn't call it home again. Not until her parents were restored to their thrones. Not until she and the Sunchaser walked the Palace gardens together. Until then it was the Shifter's Palace they journeyed to — not home.

They traveled out of the village to the main road to Balinor. Ari looked for the crossroads sign, at the junction of the Queen's highway and a narrow path that led to . . . what was it Dr. Bohnes had said? Pellian, that was it. The Manor of the House of the Fifth Lord.

The road traveled up and up. Then it dipped down to the valley where the Palace lay beside the River Fallow.

Twice during the journey, they slipped off the road and hid. The first was to avoid a party of villagers, out on some late-night errand. Chase heard them long before she did.

"Will we hide or fight?"

"Easy, Chase. I hope we won't have to fight tonight. If we do . . ." She didn't want to think about it. She and Dr. Bohnes had discussed the best way to retrieve the remainder of Chase's horn for hours. Finally, Ari had won the argument. The two of them must go alone. That way, they had the best chance of remaining hidden. And finding the final piece and slipping away in the night.

The second time, it was Ari who pulled them over into the trees.

"I hear nothing," Chase said.

"I don't hear anything, either," Ari whispered. "I just feel it. We have to get out of the way!" She rode him deep into the brush. He picked his way with care, avoiding branches, stepping into soft piles of leaves. Ari finally drew rein and sat as still as she could, listening.

"What is it, milady?"

The back of her neck prickled. A cold wind stirred. She stared up at the moon. Clouds were forming overhead, thick and sullen. The wind picked up and stirred her hair with cold, cold fingers. She scanned the sky and then jerked in alarm. There! There it was! A huge shadow crossed the moon, dimming its bright face. The shape was . . . what?

She was afraid to look, but she didn't dare look away. A winged horse — no, a unicorn. Blacker than the night sky. With burning sockets where its eyes should be.

The Shifter's Eye. Looking for them!

Ari whimpered, but bit it back. This thing had destroyed her family and home. And she would face it, someday! The terrible shadow moved back and forth, a slow sweep across the moon.

Ari buried her face in her hands, almost too scared to move. Time passed. She didn't know how much. But the cold wind died away. Night sounds returned to normal: the squeak of small mice in the grass, the whoop of a night bird hunting. She tapped her heels lightly into Chase's sides.

"Is it far now, milady?"

"A mile, maybe less."

They rode on in silence. They began to descend into the valley. Clouds covered the moon and the way was dark. A cluster of houses and shops lay just outside the Palace grounds. Some of the Royal household lived here; the farrier who shod the unicorns, the tailor in charge of the seamstresses who made the Royal family's clothes. And there was a park by a bend in the River Fallow, where Ari and her brothers used to play when they were younger.

Houses and shops were silent and dark. "No one dares to go abroad at night now," Lord Lexan had said, that long-ago day at the Unicorn Inn. "Except in armed groups." And it was so. If anyone behind the barricaded doors heard them pass, they wouldn't come out. Too many evil things stalked the night.

Chase stopped a short way from the Palace. Ari realized with a start that it was small, as Palaces go. She'd been away too long, and had seen too much of the outside world. The twin towers that guarded the front gate loomed much larger in her mind than the reality. And the moat was smaller across than she'd thought. With care, Chase could jump it.

"And so we arrive," Chase said.

Ari didn't say anything, afraid to speak aloud. A yellow-green light glowed from a window in the peak of the castle. That had been her parents' quarters. The light was sickly, disgusting. She knew who lived there now.

A slow shuffle came from the top of the wall surrounding her former home. A sentry or a guard? Coming closer.

She drew the reins out to either side of Chase's head and tapped her heels against his hindquarters. He backed up until she loosened her legs and drove her seat lightly into his back. Then she flexed her right calf, raised the right rein, and he broke into a canter, almost noiseless because of the burlap sacking on his hooves.

She checked him at the edge of the moat, rose onto his withers, and drove her heels hard into his sides. He jumped. For a moment, they hung suspended over the moat. She bit back a yell. Out of the corner of her eye, she caught a glimpse of a scaly back, a gruesome tentacle.

They landed with a thump on the other side of the moat. The shuffling overhead stopped.

Ari slipped off Chase's back and drew him into the shadows of the castle wall.

"Who goes there!" The voice was grating. Whoever it was breathed like a hissing snake. "I said, who goes there?"

"Garn!" Another voice, higher, but just as sibilant. "You find somethin'?"

Two of them. Ari's hands were cold. She had no weapon, except her father's knife. Wouldn't have another weapon until they found the rest of Chase's horn.

If they found the horn.

"Dunno," said the voice above her.

She felt, rather than saw, a pair of red-coal eyes peer over the edge of the wall.

"Maybe it's Sistern. Yo! Sistern! Want a night-time snack?" Something flew off the castle wall and landed in the moat with a splash. The water erupted with a roar. A scaly head rose from the moat. Ari couldn't see it as much as smell it. Hot breath, like a stinking furnace. Scaly arms, with claws at the ends, flailed in the air. There was a gulp! And whatever the guard threw over the wall was gone.

"Told ya, Garn. It's just before dawn. And Sistern gets hungry just before dawn."

"You think that's what I heard?"

"Sure of it."

"You got any more of what you threw to her?"

"It's been dead awhile," the guard said doubtfully. "But yeah."

"I'm a bit hungry, too. Think I'll go get me some."

"Don't you eat all of it, hear?"

"I'll eat what I can before *you* get there."

Ari heard scuffling, a few blows and snarls, and then the sound of the guards moving away. She waited until everything was quiet.

Where do we look? For one terrible moment, despair overwhelmed her. The danger was so great! It was so dark! Ari swallowed hard, collecting her thoughts.

Ari was glad she and Chase could still communicate without words. She responded with her knees, pressing him forward, guiding him around the base of the castle wall. She kept her eye on the jewel at the base of Chase's horn. It will warm, Dr. Bohnes had said, when you are close to the missing piece of the horn.

Chase jigged impatiently under her. He hated moving slowly. It wasn't in his nature. *You must let me walk on!*

Ari couldn't speak aloud. She kept light, firm hands on the reins. He balked.

She flexed the reins, right, left, right, left. He half reared, then plunged forward. She loved Chase's

113

proud spirit, but now was not the time! She did what she'd never done before and jerked hard on the reins. There was no bit in his mouth, but she knew to him it was a punishment, that she would fight him.

The ruby flared hot on Chase's forehead. He leaped forward with an eager whinny. It was loud. Too loud. Ari gasped in fear.

Above them, the guards shouted an alarm.

She jumped off the stallion's back, stumbling slightly as she landed in the dark. She turned, almost blind in the darkness, and stumbled against the wall.

She reached up and felt the ruby. Stone cold.

She started forward, her hand on the jewel. The jewel heated up. It was like some mad game of blindman's bluff. She couldn't see!

The stallion blundered along behind her, seeking the lost piece of horn as frantically as she did.

Torches flared on the castle wall. Shouts, curses, oaths streamed from the running guards.

The jewel flared hot and wild. Ari stumbled and threw her hand out to break her fall. Gravel slid underneath her hand. She fumbled desperately, her heart thudding. And there it was!

There it was, warm under her hand. The final spiral stone.

She heard the iron gate groan open, the thud of many running feet.

"Keep calm, keep calm, keep calm,"she muttered. "Bend down, Chase! Come down!" It didn't matter now that the guards heard her speak. They'd been discovered — and if she just had a little more time!

The great horse bent his neck. Trembling, she fit the spiral stones together. . . .

And there was a burst of rainbow light. It arched high and wide, tumbling the astonished guards back on their heels. It arched to the stars and back again, lighting the countryside like the most brilliant display of fireworks ever seen. It lit the guards, short, misshapen gnomes with blackened faces and wild white eyes. It lit up the great bronze horse himself.

And then, he was a horse no more. His horn sprang from his forehead like a beautiful spear. The ruby glowed at its base.

"ARIANNA!"Chase shouted. "ARIANNA! COME TO ME!"

14

✦✦✦

Ari never knew where her scarred legs got the strength. But she sprang onto her unicorn's back. Chase reared and screamed a challenge to the sky.

He turned on the gnome guards and scattered them with quick thrusts of his warrior horn. Ari clung to his back, wild laughter in her throat.

The guards scattered like leaves before the storm of the Lord of the Unicorn's wrath.

The Sunchaser leaped the moat. Ari clung to his mane. They raced into the darkness, past the darkened village, to the freedom of the forest beyond.

The night sky over Balinor was a rich river. The full moon floated there, calm and quiet. Her shining rays lit up the countryside below, flooding the road with silver light, making the forest impenetrably dark.

Ari bent low over the neck of her racing stallion, afraid to look behind. Were the grotesque guards of the Palace following? Moonlight glinted off Chase's horn. If they did follow, if they did try to pull her from the stallion's back, if she had to fight again, it was worth it! The great unicorn was whole again, his horn restored. Chase had fought the guards as if he'd been born to battle. His iron hooves had lashed out again and again. He had used his horn like a sword, thrusting and shoving the scar-faced gnomes aside. And then they had leaped the moat, springing to freedom.

Chase bent to the left, thundering around the curve in the road that took them away from the Palace. Ari felt the stallion shudder. His head dropped as his breath came in deeper gasps. She slid one hand along the side of his muscular neck and felt the sweat run through her fingers like heavy rain. She sat up and drove herself lightly into the saddle to slow him. "Easy, boy. Easy, Chase."

"We — must — get — to — the — village." His voice was deep, like a bell. But he was very close to exhaustion. She'd forgotten what his voice had sounded like, all those long months she hadn't known who she was. All those long months he couldn't speak.

"It won't help if *I* have to carry *you*," she said softly. "Come on, Chase. Walk, please. Walk."

He slowed down. She could feel him trembling. He stopped.

117

"Walk on, Chase."

"Be quiet, Arianna, and listen. I want to know if we are being followed."

"Just for a moment, Chase. You're too wet to stand in this breeze. You have to keep moving to cool off."

"A cold won't matter if we are captured."

Ari flexed the right rein and tightened her right leg against his side. Obediently, he swung in a circle, then halted, head up, ears forward, staring toward the west where the Palace lay. Ari held her breath, listening as intently as she could. A dawn breeze was coming up, rustling the leaves of the trees in the forest. There was a thrashing from the brush at one side of the road. Ari jumped and Chase moved forward in response.

"Keep still, milady."

"Sorry," she muttered. "I don't hear anything strange." She kept her voice to a whisper. "No gnomes or anything."

"And I?" He turned his head. The moonlight shimmered on his horn, glanced bright light from his eyes. His mane flowed over her knees. "I hear shouts, in the distance. From the Palace. Shouts of rage."

"Your ears are better than mine."

He didn't answer this, but she could feel him stiffen with outraged pride. Well, of *course*, he seemed to say.

Suddenly, a shriek split the air. A cry of terror. In the west, a dark shadow rose above the tops of the trees. It was huge. It blotted out the moon. Ari gasped and bent over Chase's neck, to hide in his long mane.

"Look up," he said. His voice was kind but firm. "And see what happens to those who fail the Shadow King."

Ari forced her eyes open. If Dr. Bohnes was right, if she really was the Princess, then she had to face the unfaceable. The giant shadow circled the trees. Beneath the terrifying spread of those wings, she saw a tiny figure dangling. The shriek came again, more faintly now, and then the little figure dropped, spun away, falling out of sight. The cry was cut off abruptly.

"The guard?" Ari asked, her voice shaking. "The one that didn't hear us until it was too late?"

"One of them, at least, will never guard the Palace gates again." He jerked his muzzle up. "Did you hear that? They shut the gates. I think we are safe for now."

Ari sighed. "We have to get back to the Inn, Chase. But slowly. You really do need to cool off."

The sun had poked slim pink fingers over the horizon by the time Chase and Ari returned to the Inn in Luckon. Ari had never been so tired. She slipped off Chase's back and drew him to the darkness of the barn. Except the sun seemed to have followed them inside. Or maybe that lazy Innkeeper had stuck some lanterns around. If only she could *sleep*! But she couldn't sleep until she curried Chase, put a blanket on him, and then found Dr. Bohnes and Lori. She patted Chase's neck and yawned.

"Oh, my gosh." Lori's voice was high with excitement. "Oh, my *gosh*!"

Ari's eyes flew open. "You guys waited up?"

Dr. Bohnes snorted. "Of course we waited up. We were worried sick."

Ari yawned again. "I'm *sorry*! I just can't keep my eyes open. Here, Chase, step outside for a second so they can see your horn."

"You're kidding, right?" Lori was awed. "I mean, look at him, Ari. Haven't you even looked at him?"

"Well, if you'd been chased by trolls and flying monsters and huge squi —"Ari stopped herself. She looked at her unicorn. Really *looked* at him.

Even in the darkness of the dirty barn, he glowed like a bronze moon. The elegance in his neck, shoulders, and hindquarters was like the exquisite cut of the ruby jewel.

"Hooves," grunted Dr. Bohnes. She unwound the muffling sacks from Chase's feet. The burlap seemed to fall away. His hooves were solid bronze.

"Good," Dr. Bohnes said. She rapped his right forefoot with her knuckle. "Hard as it should be. Excellent." She hoisted herself to her feet with a loud groan. "Well, milady. What do you think of the Sunchaser now? Do you see any changes?" She shot Ari a glance full of understanding. "So, then."

Ari put her hands behind her back and walked around her unicorn. He was taller, surely, and his mane longer. His tail was a silky banner, falling to the ground behind him. His eyes were a deeper brown, almost mahogany.

But they were the same eyes. Chase's eyes. Filled with warmth. Understanding. And that unbreakable spirit.

He snorted and bent his great head. She felt his breath in her hair, and flung her arms around his neck. "No," Ari said. "No changes." She kept her head hidden, so they couldn't see the tears. "He's just the same, inside." She fought for control of her voice. "So, it's over."

"Over?" Dr. Bohnes settled her glasses firmly onto her nose. "Over? Not by a long shot. Grab some grub and sleep fast, ladies. You've got another quest coming up. Right on the heels of this one."

"Uh-uh," Lori said. "No more quests. This one was enough for me, thank you very much."

"Um. What is it, exactly?" Ari asked.

"Your scepter, Your Highness. The Shifter's hidden it somewhere. And there's no finding the King and Queen until you get the scepter back."

"Scepter?" Lori said interestedly. "Royal?"

"Yep." Dr. Bohnes smiled.

"Ah — and would it be the kind of scepter that had jewels on it?"

"Quite a few, as I recall."

Lori put her arm around Ari's shoulder. "Princess, buddy, old pal," she said happily. "On with the quest!"

About the Author

Mary Stanton loves adventure. She has lived in Japan, Hawaii, and all over the United States. She has held many different jobs, including singing in a nightclub, working for an advertising agency, and writing for a TV cartoon series. Mary lives on a farm in upstate New York with some of the horses who inspire her to write adventure stories like the UNICORNS OF BALINOR.